ROMANCING THE DOCTOR

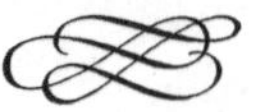

ALIE GARNETT

12-153-44 PUBLISHING

Edited by Thoth Editing

Images © iStock by Getty Images – abezikus & Christine Kohler

Cover Design © Designed with Grace

❀ Created with Vellum

This book is for my husband who puts up with me every day and didn't bat an eye when I said I wanted to write a book. Then he gave me the time to do just that. Thank you, love you too.

CHAPTER 1

Forty hours on her feet: That was what Dylan was going to blame the slight tremor on today. Maybe it was too much caffeine since coffee was the only thing fueling her now. On top of all that, Leah was working with her, and her voice grated against her nerves.

Tying off the last suture, she breathed a sigh of relief as she straightened and all the bones in her back cracked from the strain of being hunched over the young soldier for over three hours. Rolling her aching neck, she turned away, hoping he would survive.

"Vitals are good, Dr. Marquez," the rough voice stated from the monitors that were keeping track of every important function of the young man's body. There were no monitors to tell them what he was thinking, feeling, or missing, though.

"Thank you, Leah." She acknowledged her words though she knew that based on the beeping coming from the machines, everything was good. After being at this for over a dozen years, there was little that she wasn't aware of when she was in the OR. Most of the time, she was more comfortable here than in her own living room—hell, it was all the time.

"Did you want me to talk to his CO, Dr. Marquez?" Elissa was already heading out the door to speak to the commanding officer as she said the words, knowing that Dylan never went out to talk to those who were waiting on the outcome of the mess that was brought to her.

"Yes, please." Turning back to the kid on her table, she looked at his face for the first time. Her entire concentration had been on his leg for the hours they had been together, or where his leg used to be. Looking at the man or woman wasn't something she usually did. It didn't matter—her job was to save his life. Once her job was done, she was never going to see them again; post-op was done by others, or they were sent to better facilities far from the war zone they had been injured at. She just got another mutilated body to rebuild as best she could.

Pulling off her bloody gloves, she turned away from the blond kid whose life was completely different today than it was yesterday. As with everyone she saw, her job wasn't to deal with minor scratches; it was usually to save a life.

After giving orders for medication and a recommendation as to where he should be sent, she headed to the locker room to clean up. Once the adrenaline was gone, fatigue would set in quickly. Her shift today had run long, and her body knew it.

In the quiet, empty room, she sat heavily on the metal bench. Exhaustion hit hard as her butt hit the seat, like it knew the day was over. Forty hours was too long to be working; she knew that. But when the day was full of maimed and broken soldiers, and the medical staff was short, you did as much as you could.

Resting her hands on her knees, she could see that they were shaking. Not just the slight tremble that had overtaken them in the operating room, but a full-on shake. Squeezing them into tight fists, she demanded that they stop. They were her tools to use, and they did not control her.

"Dylan, the CO wants to talk to you," Elissa said from the doorway. Had she seen the shaking?

Glancing at her nurse, she was happy she had been assigned the young woman. Bubbly, cheerful, and people-person, Elissa was also top-notch at her job. She would be sent home in a few months, and Dylan would get another nurse but didn't think she would find one she like as much as Elissa.

Forcing her fists to relax, she asked the blond, "Why?"

It wasn't an odd question; most of the officers were alright with learning what happened from a nurse. Rarely did they push to actually talk to her, mostly because she had no time to rehash what she had done to one soldier, only to do it again a few minutes later to another.

"Let's do it then." Not letting the woman answer, she got up, pushing off sleep for another few minutes. Being so used to sleep deprivation should have bothered her, but she no longer noticed it.

"I can talk to him again," Elissa suggested. She could probably tell Dylan was about to drop or maybe she saw the tremor in Dylan's hands. But Elissa had been by her side for nearly the entire forty hours, and she was ready to drop also.

"No, you go home." Dylan pushed her friend farther into the locker room on her way out.

Not that either would be heading "home" after their shift; they would both head for the barracks that they were housed in during their time in the desert. There was nothing homey about it. It was just a place to go in your off hours as you waited to go home at the end of your tour.

Stepping out into the hallway, she dreaded talking to the officer. It seemed she could never get enough emotion into it. Remembering that the man on her table was a human and not just another patient was hard. Soon she pushed her way into the small and seldom-frequented visitor area. Family never came this close to the war zone. Friends were your best bet, but they couldn't take time off to be with the injured— they were fighting a war too.

Realizing she was still in her gauzy blue protective layer, she pulled off the top that was still covered in the blood of the friend of whoever she was going to talk to. The material tore easily, and she balled it in her hands, hoping he didn't notice what it was. Blood was a part of her everyday routine, but not everyone else's.

From the corner, a man unfolded himself from one of the few uncomfortable chairs in the small room. Nobody else was there, so he must be who she was looking for. He was tall and his presence filled the room, making it seem even smaller.

Taking a moment, she looked him over from his closely shorn head of dark hair to the Army-issue boots that were the exact same as hers and everyone else around. His fatigues fit far better than most, though. Not that she was noticing, she was working after all.

If she hadn't been awake for nearly two days, she would have thought he was handsome. He was older than the soldier on her table by close to a decade, and from the weariness in his eyes, most of those years were probably spent here and not with his family back home.

"I'm Major Marquez." She went straight to him, holding out her hand. She had long stopped saying 'doctor' in her introductions—everyone she talked to knew who she was.

His warm hand engulfed hers and sent an odd tingle up her arm. Lack of sleep was making everything feel strange lately. She was too tired to try and examine those feelings but quickly pulled her hand away from his.

"Hello, Major," his deep cool voice said as he dropped his hand. His eyes were on her, and he actually looked her up and down. Not that he would find anything that exceptional; she was in loose scrubs and was still covered in blue gauze. Even her dark hair was hidden away in a braid, and she half-wondered if there was still a protective hat on her head.

"Private Jackson lost his right leg, just below the knee. He will be transferred—" she started, her usual explanation of the injuries and what she did to them. Then she'd get into what would be happening to the soldier now that she was done with him.

"The nurse told me that already," he interrupted her. "I wanted to see you."

"Oh, okay."

"You're Jessica Dylannski?" he said a name she barely recognized anymore.

Who had been the last person to call her that name? Right now, she couldn't even remember. She had been Dylan for fifteen years. Flicking her eyes down his uniform, she read his name, the one she didn't pay attention to—it usually didn't matter. Captain Marquez...the same as hers.

"Not in a long time, Captain," she admitted, probably because her brain was shutting down. This was too much information after no sleep.

"Chase was my older brother," the man said, making Dylan's heart stop. It had been years since that name had passed anyone's lips in her presence.

Somewhere in the back of her mind, she recalled Chase talking about his younger brothers. Had there been three of them? Four? She couldn't remember anymore, but it seemed one had followed his footsteps into the Army. And then found her.

"I don't know what to say to you," was all she could say as she turned to leave. There was nothing for them to talk about. She had nothing to say to anyone from Chase's family, hadn't in fifteen years.

"I had heard about a Doc Marquez and wanted to see if it was really you. You've changed." His words stopped her.

Turning, she looked at him, trying to find the boy she had loved in his features; they were brothers after all. Seeing nothing, she said, "Have I ever met you?"

Though they had been together for four years, she had never gone home with Chase and was never introduced to his family. Back then, she never wanted to be.

"At the funeral."

"I didn't meet anyone that day. You all pretended I didn't exist, or worse."

"As I seem to recall, you didn't do anything to ingratiate yourself with us."

"I'm sorry, Captain, I should have thought about *your* feelings that day. I should have just forgotten every awful thing your mother had said to me over the years and forgave everyone for hating me. What was I thinking? Oh yeah! I was burying my fucking husband!" She whirled around on him and stomped from the room.

Suddenly, her hands were shaking for a completely other reason, no longer from fatigue or caffeine or even the burnout she was completely terrified of. Now, it was her past running her down and reminding her that she was nothing and never would be.

Chase Marquez had been the love of her life. Alone and happy, they had said they would love each other until the end of time. A month later, it all came to an end with his death. Since that day, she had pushed herself to become a doctor and then focused everything on her job.

Now she was just short of forty, and her body was starting to fail her. If she lost that, her life was over… She had nothing.

CHAPTER 2

OLD ANGER ROLLED through Holden as he watched her storm away from him. Her lower half covered in a blue gauze that was covered in blood still, and her upper in a soft gray scrub top, also with hints of blood on it. *Jackson's blood or someone else's?*

It was true she hadn't been what he'd expected, but he couldn't remember much from the funeral of his hero. What little there was held nothing of the woman who they had learned after his brother's death was his wife.

Not that Chase talked much about her the few times he was home, but Holden knew they had been together for four years. Meeting in basic training and falling hard, but Donna Marquez didn't want her son in the Army and didn't want him to find love there either. For years she told Chase his choice was not good, which led him to marry Jessica in secret before he deployed for the last time.

Holden's only actual memory of the woman before the funeral was a snapshot his brother left behind of them together in basic. Arm in arm and smiling, Chase was tall, young, and handsome. His brother had his whole life in front of him and his buddy by his side. She was shorter back then, blond and plumper than he had thought his brother would like, even after all these years.

At the funeral, his mother had taken Chase's stuff, things that should have gone to his wife, but nobody was about to tell Donna she wasn't allowed to have her son's stuff. Jessica had watched her and said nothing. By then, she had grown a few more inches and had lost her plumpness, her hair the dark brown it was today.

When his mother had grabbed the folded flag from Jessica's arms—the moment it was set there—Jessica had just dropped her arms and let it happen. At the time, he was only sixteen, but even he knew his mother was in the wrong.

After the funeral, he hadn't seen or heard from her again until three months ago when he started to hear about a Doc J. D. Marquez. It had taken him time to make the connection since his brother had never called her Jessica, always Dylan, a short form of her last name, Dylannski.

After a little research, he found out his brother's wife had stayed in school and became a doctor. According to the name she went by, she either never remarried or had kept Chase's name.

Today, his crew had been on a mission that had went south, and Jackson had been taken to the medical center. He was the first of his team to get wounded this badly. The kid had lost a leg; his military career had just started, and now it was over.

When he was told that Dr. Marquez was operating on Jackson, Holden knew he had to see her. Just once. He hadn't even planned to tell her who he was, but he wanted to talk to her about his brother. It had been so long, and he wanted to know what the man was really like. He had been sixteen when his brother had died, but he had only been twelve when he joined up. The age gap had been enough that Holden hadn't known his brother well.

Chase joining the Army was a surprise—they were a Navy family, and everyone was expected to join the Navy. Chase, however, wanted to join the Army and become a Ranger. Even though Holden had two other brothers who did join the Navy, he knew that he was going to be a Ranger like his brother.

After leaving the hospital, Holden couldn't get her blue eyes out his mind. They were blank and cool as she talked about Jackson, just another soldier that she worked on. But those same cool blues had flashed with pain at his brother's name, even after all these years.

She was right—they should have worked to include her in the family. But as far as he knew, she and Chase had never made a point of visiting or being a part of the family. But he had been a kid and maybe hadn't known everything going on.

"How's Jackson?" Luke Gregory asked as soon as Holden got to their group. Everyone was lounging on their beds, waiting for news.

"Alive. Lost a leg, but he's going home." He made it sound like it was a good thing, but it was a devastating injury.

"Lucky bastard," Luke mumbled.

"No, Gregory, he lost a fucking *leg!*" he yelled at the younger man. Jackson was only lucky that he hadn't died.

"Of course," Luke replied under his breath, leaving the group in a huff.

"Did you get to see Dr. Sexy Marquez?" Kyle Sanchez asked from his bed, his eyebrows wagging.

"You mean the doctor that saved Jackson's life? Yes, I saw her." He sat heavily on his bed.

Kyle had it right about how sexy that woman was. Even with the scars on her chin and jaw, she was striking. His brother had been a lucky man. None of his memories had her as hot as she was, and how his fifteen-year-old self couldn't see that, he didn't know.

"Jackson got to have her hands all over him? Luck shit," Kyle groaned and leaned back against his bunk.

"He was most likely not conscious as it happened." Holden unbuttoned his shirt, too many layers for the heat.

"Her hands could bring me back from dead." Kyle looked at his own hands.

"That's what her job is." He shook his head at the man. The woman was a doctor; every day, she saved lives.

Kyle rolled on his side to face him since the other guys were mostly not paying attention, saying, "I heard she's horny as *hell.*"

"What?" He didn't want to hear it, but he did. The few minutes he had been with her, she hadn't sent him that vibe at all, but it might have been tempered by the dark circles under her eyes.

"Rumor has it that she's an easy lay. Sleeps around quite a bit. But then again, she *is* a doctor, and they do that around here," Kyle surmised after his three months of knowledge of desert life.

"I don't know about that, but she saved Jackson, and that's all that matters." He laid down and wondered about his sister-in-law.

Could it be true that she slept around? It didn't matter; she was a widow and had been for a long time. But it still bothered him that his brother could be that forgettable, that she would sleep with just anyone.

"I'd tap that," Kyle said as he rolled onto his back, looking at the ceiling.

"Why don't you concentrate on staying alive and not on women who're out of your league, Sanchez," he reminded the younger man. Hell, the woman was almost a decade older than he was, and Sanchez was even younger than him.

"An older woman could teach me some stuff, sir." The young man grinned.

"She would chew you up, and you'd *still* be worthless in the sack." He laughed at the younger man's pained expression.

CHAPTER 3

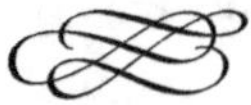

YEARS AGO, after basic training, Dylan had taken to running to shed the pounds she'd easily gain if she wasn't always fighting against it. It worked, and even though she couldn't run every day, she ran as much as possible. Those were the days she pushed herself to her limits, adding miles whenever she could. Once her lungs were burning and her mind was clean, she could stop. Until then, she ran.

Walking into the dorm-like building that she had been living in for two years, she headed up the stairs. Her watch told her that she had run close to sixteen miles this time, multiple laps around the hospital complex.

For years her mother toggled between telling her it was just baby fat and being big-boned, but neither had been the truth. Before, she had just been lazy. So lazy, she struggled hard at the shear amount of physical activity in basic training. In the few months she had been there, she had lost close to twenty pounds and had gained muscle she hadn't known was possible. Twenty years later, she was still maintaining it.

Dylan had slept for over twelve hours, but now she was up and ready to start another day. Sadly, she was still off for a few hours after being written up for working too many hours in a week.

She had journals to read and paperwork to catch up on, so that would have to keep her busy for now. At this point in her life, she had no hobbies and found it hard to find good friends when work kept her so busy. Then there was the constant turnover of people as some went home and new ones arrived.

A moment later, she opened the door to her tiny apartment—actually, it was just a room for sleeping. There was no kitchen or living room, just a bed and desk. Food was served at the canteen, and there were couches on the first floor to enjoy. This was a place to sleep.

Grabbing a towel and her toiletries, she headed out to take a long shower. She heard her name being called as she started down the hall for the facilities.

"Major Marquez," the voice said, a voice she had somehow remembered from the short conversation she had with him the day before. Captain Holden Marquez.

"Afternoon, Captain," she said brightly, more brightly than she actually felt.

Turning and facing him, she was disappointed that he was just as handsome now than when she was sleep deprived. Not that she was attracted to him…he was Chase's brother, after all.

"I just wanted to tell you I'm sorry about yesterday. I was rude, and you didn't deserve that." His eyes were friendly today, so different from the day before.

"Apology excepted. Thank you, Captain." She smiled, but she didn't feel it.

"Holden, you can call me Holden. I'm, uh, also sorry about before. Jessica, I wish I could go back and change things." His hand extended between them. *A peace offering?*

"It's Dylan. I don't go by Jessica anymore, and don't worry about the past; it's over." She hugged the towel closer to her, not taking the hand he was offering. Mostly because of the weirdness of the last time she shook hands; she didn't need to experience that in a wakeful state.

"Chase would have wanted…" He dropped the hand as he spoke.

"Do not tell me what you think he would have wanted, Captain. Nobody cared about what he wanted then, so don't pretend to know what he would want now. I have to take a shower—excuse me."

"He probably doesn't want to know how his wife turned out, either," he hissed. Obviously, her words had hit their mark.

"What is that supposed to mean?" she demanded, turning on him.

"It means that you're pretty loose with your morals."

"Excuse me?"

"You heard me. Chase wouldn't like to know his wife sleeps around," he sneered.

"Do not talk like you have any idea who I am or who he was. Your family didn't think I was good enough to love him, but now demands that I mourn him for the rest of my life?" She knew her knuckles were white with strain from clenching her fists.

"Maybe seeing that he meant something to you would be enough."

"Sorry I stopped wearing black, so you couldn't see me in them fifteen years later. But I had to learn to live again—guess I succeeded." Closing her eyes, she knew she wasn't getting to the shower. She was going to break down, and she wasn't doing that in a public bathroom.

"*Very* successful," he spit at her.

"You're as much of an ass as the rest of them." She turned back to her room, checking him in the shoulder on her way.

"Aren't you going to shower?" he asked.

"Not anymore. I have to mourn my husband some more."

"I thought you said you were done with that?"

Still walking down the hall, she said evenly, "Marquez was my life. He died at 2:08 a.m. my time. I woke from a dead sleep and knew he was gone. Don't tell me I didn't love him enough. *Ever.*"

Without looking at him, she walked into her room and slammed the door behind her. Dropping everything in her hands, she sank to the floor as her body started to shake.

Chase Marquez had been her world for the four years they had together. He was her biggest cheerleader when she needed one the most. Without him, she wouldn't be where she was today. He had encouraged her to become a doctor—when she had doubted her ability, he never had.

Back when she had enlisted, she had said that she would do anything in the Army but wanted to be a nurse one day. Her recruiter had pushed and had said that based on her grades in school, she should think about being a doctor. The Army would pay for schooling, she just had to have the brains.

Two months before her high school graduation, she got on a bus for Alabama and sat next to another kid from town who had gone to the other high school. They got to know each other during the long drive, and Marquez had told her she would be a great doctor, something those who swore they loved her didn't think she was capable of.

She had fallen hard for him, and he had felt the same. Not once did they not feel that they were going to be together forever. Even with them both in the Army, they fought for time together.

After boot camp, they had gone their separate ways: her to college in Florida and him to Iraq for his first tour. Through calls and letters, they kept their love alive. Knowing he would be deployed again soon, he went to her when he was stateside, not his parents.

Though he had told his parents about Jessica, they didn't want to know her. That wasn't the only reason she didn't visit them. His parents never realized the two had the same hometown, and she refused to go back.

Chase was gearing up for his second deployment when he had insisted they get married. At first she had been resistant; she was busy with school and didn't want to make his parents hate her any more than they already did. But she hadn't been able to dissuade him, and they had married in front of a judge with two county employees as witnesses.

A month later he was gone, shot by a sniper. She had never told anyone before that she knew he was dead when it happened, choosing to keep that to herself. But Holden had made it sound like she wasn't still mourning Marquez, as if it would only take fifteen years to get over the love of her life.

As if when she closed her eyes, she didn't hear him say, "Love you, Dylan." He was the first to call her that, and she had taken it as her name after his death. No longer was she Jessica D., now she was J. Dylan.

After he was gone, all she had to focus on was getting her PhD. Then her world became about saving lives and being the best at what she did.

Holden was right, though. She slept around. She was a woman who enjoyed sex. It wasn't as if Marquez was coming back; they were separate forever. After fifteen years, she had not been in another relationship because she couldn't love another like she had loved him. Didn't even want to.

Getting off the floor, she crawled into her bed and closed her eyes, ignoring the fact that she smelled of sweat and had sand all over her. Curling into a tight ball, she let her mind go back to a time when she was loved and thought nothing could take that away, with her husband's arms tight around her.

CHAPTER 4

DEEP, deep darkness was replaced by light, bright light that hurt his eyes. From somewhere in the distance, a new voice stated, "Welcome back, Captain."

"W-what?" was all he could choke out though his dry mouth.

"You were ambushed and got shot. But the bullet didn't go to deep, and the doc got it out. Sorry to say you'll probably be staying here for a while. Recovery will be quick, though, and then it's back to work for you." The blonde nurse was cheery as she talked about the gore of war and piled little tools onto a tray.

"My men?" he asked, because he couldn't remember. His vision finally came back into focus. He was in a recovery room. *What the hell happened?*

"All are good. You were the only one injured today." She actually patted him on the head.

"Thank you," he said in confusion.

"Don't thank me, I didn't do much. Dr. Marquez did all the hard work," the woman replied, smiling at him.

It had been over a month since he had last seen her, or at least talked to her. He had seen her a few times, running in her dirty sneakers and gray shorts. It seemed once he noticed her that first time, he had noticed her every time since.

Seeing her in shorts and a T-shirt had been completely different from seeing her all covered in gauze and scrubs. The formerly white, now desert-gray running shoes below her long, lean legs. She'd somehow even made the Army-issued shorts and T-shirt sexy as she did laps around the hospital.

What had made him mad about the entire conversation was that he was attracted to her, more than he really wanted to admit. She was his brother's widow, and he was attracted to her.

"Can I thank her?" he asked.

"No, she's already gone. IED got five today, so she'll be in surgery for hours. I will be there soon."

"Did she know it was me?" He wanted to know. Maybe she wouldn't have worked on him if she had.

"I don't know, she doesn't always look. Another body is another body; they blend after a time. Her goal is just to save them all." She peeled her bloody gloves off.

"Does she?" He was beginning to think she was a miracle worker.

"No, nobody saves them all. We do our best though. Do you know her?" She pulled off her glasses and cleaned the blood off them with her shirt, only to get more on them than was on there before.

"Not well, really. She worked on a guy under me last month," he explained, not knowing how much this woman knew about her or how much he should reveal.

"Shoot, I thought you were one of her conquests. So far, we haven't had one of those come through here. Or, if we have, she's never said. We don't get a lot of talkers." The woman chuckled at her observation.

"Conquests?" He pretended to not know what she was talking about.

"Dr. Marquez likes a good one-night stand. It's as regulated as her surgery schedule. I'm sure her lovers are told what to do every step of the way, same as I am."

"Kind of cold, huh?"

"I doubt it. She just knows what she wants and needs, then makes it happen and leaves."

"Nobody's good enough?" he asked with a grin, seeing that about her.

"Nobody can live up to a ghost, but it's fun to see them try."

"Ghost?"

"However many years later, and she still wears his ring? *Nobody* can compete with that."

"I didn't notice a ring." He scraped his memory for signs of a ring. He would have looked; he was sure of it.

"Then you haven't slept with her." The woman laughed at him as she patted his arm. "It's on a necklace; she never takes it off."

Closing his eyes, he wished the pain that had just raced through him was because he had been shot and not because he had been an ass. When he had accused her of getting over his brother, she was probably still wearing his ring.

Why didn't she just say that? Why did she let him believe she was over Chase, when she was still grieving? Or was the ring a cover and an excuse for her actions?

CHAPTER 5

"SORRY ABOUT NUNEZ," Elissa stated as she met back up with Dylan in her office. Both had showered and changed into clean scrubs. Elissa had taken a little time and dried her hair, whereas Dylan didn't want to waste the time and had just put it up in a ponytail, still wet.

Signing her name to another form she looked up at her in question, names were not something she paid much attention to. She knew soldiers by their wounds, not names.

"Double leg amputee," Elissa clarified without missing a beat, because it had been over a year.

"Oh, him. He had lost so much blood on the way in, and I couldn't get him back together fast enough." She knew that Elissa knew this already; she had been by her side for the surgery. But Dylan still needed to hear that there was no saving him. When she lost a patient, that meant someone else lost them as well. Someone more important than she was.

"So, I talked to the patient that got shot in the leg. He asked about you." Elissa leaned against her desk as she spoke.

"Hope you told him I was married and pregnant. Men hate that," Dylan said, as she did every time. *She* picked the men she slept with, not the other way around.

"I forgot to mention your delicate condition. How far along should I say?" Elissa teased her.

"At least six months…and showing."

"Next time. But this guy was cute." Elissa grinned at her.

"I don't remember him," she lied. The entire time she was working, she knew it was Holden Marquez because her fingers wouldn't stop tingling. By the time she had sewn him shut, she had to stop herself from caressing his otherwise perfect thigh.

"Captain Marquez, same as you… You worked on someone under him last month," Elissa said. Judging by the look on her face, Elissa couldn't remember which soldier it was though.

"Left leg amputee. Jackson," Dylan provided.

"You do remember him! You thought he was cute too." Nothing got past Elissa.

"He's young and not my type."

"Young, maybe. Let's see." Elissa flipped through the folders on Dylan's desk. Finding the right one, she opened it, saying, "Thirty-one, just right if you ask me. Why do so many guys get younger women? We need to go for younger men!"

"Says the woman who's happily married to an older man."

"Just lucked out that Todd was a senior, just read my ninth grade diary." Elissa giggled at the memory of her younger self.

"You and your high school romance. How is he doing with Ryan this time?" Elissa had been on tour three times now and loved it. Well, all of it except not having her family close by. She missed her husband Todd, and their son, Ryan.

"Better this time, I think, because he doesn't have to change diapers. My mom and sister have really stepped it up. Maybe they knew he couldn't do it after his mom passed last year, but it's like *wow* this time." Elissa explained it was the first time they had been here together, but had bonded fast. Though they were complete opposites, it was fun having a friend close by.

They wouldn't have been friends if they were stateside. She would have her husband and son, and Dylan had an empty apartment because she wasn't stateside long enough to have anything permanent.

But here, they were more equal. Neither would be here forever, their tours acting as a sort of limbo time for both of them.

"Good it hear. Everyone has to chip in to make it easier for him." Dylan gave her advice, which meant nothing. In reality, she had been alone when Marquez has left. Not many people knew he had passed away, and she didn't talk about it. There was no family to help her through the hard times on either side.

"Phone sex helps, especially with FaceTime. *Hot!*" Elissa's grin made it seem like it had recently happened.

"TMI, TMI!" she said to her friend, grabbing the file from her hand.

She opened it and instantly saw his picture. He looked less like an ass in photos. His brown eyes weren't as mad either.

Thankfully, she hadn't seen him since the day outside her room. Whether he had been avoiding her or they just didn't run in the same circles, she didn't know. She was just happy it hadn't happened.

"Hot, right?" Elissa said, looking at the picture from over her shoulder.

She continued to read the file, ignoring both the picture and her friend. He was single, and his address was either his mother's house or just in the same town. Emergency contacts were his mother and a brother named Roark. His father wasn't listed… Did that mean he was dead or just not listed?

Marquez and his father Glenn had butted heads more often than not when Dylan had known him. The older man couldn't hide his disappointment over his son joining the Army and not the Navy. She wondered if Holden had the same issue with the man. She hoped not.

"Why don't you do rounds and have another look? He doesn't disappoint." Elissa pointed at the file.

"He's a *patient*," she reminded the other woman.

"For now, but he's going to get better. Fully mobile and fully functional. Not that I looked, but I see things." Elissa winked at her.

"Was that before or after phone sex?"

"Hey! I just noticed, okay? I didn't touch it, but you can." Elissa mimicked caressing a penis.

Dylan rolled her eyes, but she couldn't help but laugh. "Why do I even talk to you?"

"Because you are the straight man, I am the crazy partner. Now go talk to the sexy guy and tell me all the details about it later. That way, I'll have more to talk about with Todd than blood and gore." She grabbed the folder back and looked it over again, mostly at the picture.

"You tell your husband about me?" Dylan demanded, realizing she had no idea who this man actually was.

"Just the good stuff, and he loves you too. You're coming over for Christmas the first year we're both back."

Dylan wondered when that would be—years from now, most likely. It had been a long time since she had been stateside for the holidays. She wished she had known Elissa back then. The one time was home, she had ended up at the hospital she was working at, it was so lonely in her apartment. Holidays were always the hardest, especially when she wasn't working.

"Count on it," she promised, taking the folder back and tucking it under her arm. She wondered if their friendship would survive after leaving the war zone.

CHAPTER 6

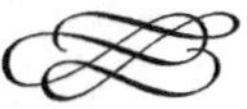

"I'M FINE, Mom, just a little gunshot wound," Holden said as he stared at the giant bandage on his leg. It was throbbing like a mean son of a bitch.

"No gunshot is small." His mother's words sounded distant. The hulking building that had been turned into a hospital didn't offer great cell reception.

"I'm okay, seriously. They're not even sending me home," he reminded her, wishing he hadn't even called her.

"They need to send you home to heal! The Navy would, you know."

"I will be healed before I even make it back. By next week, I should be back on duty. I can barely feel it," he lied to her.

"Just ask to come home, they don't need you."

"I have to go, Mom. I'll call you soon," he said and quickly hung up; his mom could say goodbye for hours.

Closing his eyes, Holden let out a long sigh. He hated calling his mother. She had been against him enlisting in the Army since the beginning and wasn't afraid to say it. And she did say it—a lot.

"Lying to your mom, huh? Isn't there a law against that?" Dylan smiled from the doorway. He wondered how long she had been there.

"More like bending the truth," he replied. For some reason, he was actually happy to see her smile.

"How are you feeling? For real." She put on her doctor's face, which matched the gray scrubs that covered her body. No blood on them today.

"Hurts, but I suspected it would." He shrugged. He was shot, after all, not pinched.

Without any hesitation, she ran her hands over the white bandage, the one her nurse put on after the surgery. She deftly pulled on thin plastic gloves and peeled back the bandage from his leg. As he watched her, he wished the wound was a few inches more away from his penis. Looking at her scrunching up her nose as she looked at his wound made him feel a little defensive.

Her plastic-covered fingers brushed his stitches, then probed the area around the wound for a while, checking for any sign of infection or excessive swelling. Then, just as fast, she placed a new bandage over the wound. She hadn't said a word, just concentrated on the job in front of her.

Watching her pull off her gloves, he said, "I thought you would have let me die after what I said."

Giving him a half-smile as she tossed her gloves away, she replied, "Marquez would've killed me if I'd let his brother die. You owe your brother for this one."

"Why do you call him Marquez?" He had noticed it right away. In all their conversations, she hadn't said his actual name.

Her eyes went to the window for a moment, then back to him. "During basic, we were just friends, so we started to call each other by our last names, just like everyone else. Things got more personal as training went on, but we kept the last name thing. Neither of us knew what the future held or if we could even make a relationship work. We did, but the last name thing just sort of stuck. I don't think of him as Chase; I never did."

"Even after you got married and were a Marquez also?" He liked listening to her talk. She relaxed when she did.

"I guess we weren't married long enough for it to be an issue. If he had come home, that might have changed." She folded her arms, a protective gesture if he ever saw one. "Anyway, you're healing well. At this point, I see you in here another three days, then out but off-duty for a week. After that, you'll be part-time, working toward full."

"That's what the other doctor said." He smiled when he saw her flinch, realizing he knew she had no reason to be there.

She started toward the door. "Okay, then. Good luck on recovery."

"Can I get you back as a doctor in case the new guy wants me dead? No brother making sure I am alive."

"Sorry, I'm usually not post-op, and I'm off for forty-eight in a few hours. You'll be out by the time I get back." She stopped at the door.

"Visit me when you're off? You can't run *all* the time," he teased her. As long as he held his tongue, it appeared that they could get along.

"We don't have anything to talk about." Her hands slipped into her pockets. *Was she being shy?*

"You can tell me about Chase. I was so young, I didn't really know him. I want to know more. You know more."

"I'll see how I feel tomorrow. Maybe," she answered and walked from the room.

He felt the conversation had been a success; they hadn't yelled at each other, at least. Add to that a genuine smile, not just a fake one today.

Holden ran his hand over the bandage that she had put on him. He hoped she hadn't noticed his erection as she had checked out his wound—he didn't see her that way and didn't want that getting in the way of learning more about his brother's life.

CHAPTER 7

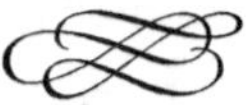

WITH NOTHING better to do with her time, Dylan headed over to the hospital after she had finally slept the night before. It wasn't losing the soldier that had kept her up longer than it should have; it was Holden. Finding him wounded, she hadn't hesitated to treat him. It was simply her job, and a body was a body, no matter what that body thought of her. But afterward in his room… That was something she had never done before. Sewing them up was easy. Pleasant conversation was something she had never mastered, never really needed to.

It didn't take any of the years of schooling she had gone through to realize he'd had an erection as she checked his wound. Elissa had been right about it being worth a glance. *Definitely impressive,* she thought to herself.

She regretted her decision even as her feet led her toward Holden's room. Since she was off duty, she was wearing her usual off-duty uniform, which was a gray Army T-shirt, one of many she had with her. After twenty years, she was more comfortable in fatigues than jeans.

Her Army-issue boots were nearly silent as she went down the quiet hallway. Nobody paid much attention to her as she went. This was her domain, and there was no reason to wonder why she'd be there on her day off. Nobody'd guess, however, that she was visiting her brother-in-law.

At this point in her life, she didn't even see him as that. He was more like just another soldier. Their connection to a man long dead didn't mean anything. Even at this point, she couldn't tell you which of his brothers Holden was, and there had been only two of them. Three of them?

She stopped at his door, knocking loudly. His eyes had been closed, and she regretted waking him, hoping his leg wasn't bothering him today.

"Doc." He smiled but didn't lift his head from the pillow as he spoke.

"Captain." Dylan took a step into the room. She took a look around, making sure everything was as it should be. Seeing that he was no longer hooked up to any machines and seemed to be in good spirits, she was relieved, realizing that she had been worried about him. Dylan pushed the thought out of her mind as she went to the row of cabinets and reached into the box of gloves.

Without thinking, she slid them on and quickly checked his wound again, happy with the progress. She re-bandaged it, then pulled off the gloves and tossed them in the corner trashcan. Today, he had no reaction to her being there. *Had that just been a fluke? Am I imagining things?*

"No infection; looks like everything's healing as it should." She couldn't help giving him a progress report—it was ingrained in her.

"I had a great surgeon." He raised his bed so he was sitting up.

"If you were sleeping, I can come back." She took a step away from the bed, gesturing to the door with her thumb.

"No, just resting. Bored. I'm happy you're here."

"Have you gotten up today?" she quizzed him.

"The evil nurse makes me every time I have to pee." He grinned.

She crossed her arms. "Good, you need to move around."

"Do you want to sit?" He waved at an uncomfortable-looking chair in the corner of the room.

"No thank you. I'll stand." She didn't want to be too comfortable around him.

"Okay. I forget you're actually in the Army." He nodded at her clothes.

"A major. In a few months, I'll have been in for twenty years," she admitted, but it didn't seem that long to her.

"Are you retiring?" he asked. She would have her years in soon.

"No, I have no plans for that. I'll most likely stay until they kick me out." She leaned against the cabinetry that ran along the wall at the foot of his bed.

"Did Chase like the Army?"

For a moment, she had forgotten why she was there. It wasn't just a patient visit, it was a dredge through her past. A past she hated talking and thinking about.

"Yes, he loved it. Even loved coming here. Truthfully, he wasn't supposed to have been in Iraq when he died. He volunteered to come back early due to troop shortages. Your mother doesn't know that. He went because I would start med school while he was gone and would have been busy. He decided it was better to be gone when I had no time than when I would have had more time to spend with him. All of it was for more time." She bit back tears. He had asked one stupid question, and she was going a bawl like a baby.

"Mom likes to say he wasn't happy with the Army and that he regretted his decision." Holden admitted it sounded like a woman who was disappointed in her oldest child.

"Your mom lied to you."

"That's what I always thought. She bends things to look the way she wants them to."

"Marquez had a hard time with your mother. She wasn't happy with his life choices. The Army, me, not moving home between every deployment..."

Holden nodded. "Yeah, she likes everyone to live close to her."

"I know, they argued about it often. I was in Florida and couldn't just pick up and leave. She didn't think I was going to get through my program, figuring I was just looking to get out of actually being deployed by getting pregnant or something. As if the Army would care about either of those things." She chuckled at the woman who had thought she was so smart about why Dylan was with Chase.

"You signed a contract. You were in."

"Still am. I keep signing on that damn dotted line."

"Did your parents at least like Chase?" he asked.

"They never met him. I was estranged from them at the time," she said it as succinctly as possible, not wanting more questions about her —this was about Marquez.

"Sorry about that. You two went at it all alone. I wish I had known."

"You were a kid; it wasn't your place," she reminded him, offering a small smile.

"Where's home when you aren't here?" he asked.

"Wherever I land. I don't have a home base. I'm usually in the DC area but have been in California, Texas, and New York. Mostly, I'm here, in the desert. Right now, I've been here for twenty-three months with no plans to leave."

"That's a long time."

"I keep getting by the medical board." She flexed her hands involuntarily; they didn't always listen to her anymore, but she hoped they held out for a few more years.

"But this is a stressful place."

"Ever been in the ER in Detroit? I had more gunshot wounds there then here on any given day. Fewer limb amputations, but the shotgun wounds made up for it." She shook her head in disappointment—she was never going back there.

"Why were you in Detroit?"

She shrugged. "I had a few months off a few years ago and took a three-month gig. I have trouble dealing with downtime." It was the absolute truth. She couldn't just sit at home, she'd do anything but that. Which was why she was still here in the sandbox.

"What did Chase like to do on his off-time?"

"Fishing, hiking…just about anything outside. If he was trapped inside, he was crawling the walls. We were alike that way." She was relieved to talk about Marquez again.

"That's what I remember also. He was never actually at the house when he came home, always out and about."

"Yep, that was him. His big plan was to hike the entire Appalachian

Trail before I got my doctorate. He had started and was probably going to finish it. I always worried when he went; he was doing it alone, and it made me nervous." As she talked, she saw his eyelids droop, the medication was making him tired. So, she kept talking, hoping it put him to sleep. "Not that I ever told him that. Every time I told him I was nervous about something, he would give me the biggest hug to 'squeeze the fear out of me.' It always made me laugh and relax. It was just how he was."

After watching him sleep for a few minutes, she was again surprised that he didn't resemble his brother at all. Every once in a while, there'd be something. Maybe she didn't remember the man she loved like she thought she did.

She left the room and quietly closed the door behind her. Holden needed sleep more than talking about his long-dead brother. Back down the hall, she still didn't get any unusual looks.

It had been nice talking about Marquez, remembering him. Usually, she spent her time trying not to remember life with him, trying to make the way her life was now seem normal and not just a poor substitute for the life she couldn't get back again.

Looking back on it, she knew she was painting life with a rose-colored brush. Was it possible that they never fought? Were they always happy, even when separated for months at a time?

Of course not. They hated being separated, but they both accepted it because that was their normal. They were Army—they would rarely be together until their careers ended. They weren't happy about it, but both had accepted it.

They were young, passionate people with big opinions, and they fought all the time. Over what, she could barely remember. The only thing was his family and hers. His family was easy, they weren't happy with them as a couple. Hers wasn't so, she had cut them from her life at eighteen. By the time she got on that bus for basic she was alone, joining the Army had given her a family. They may not be close, but it was a family.

CHAPTER 8

Two o'clock passed, and Dylan hadn't come back. For some reason, he expected her to come back today. Holden cursed himself for falling asleep while she was talking, but it was her fault for having such a soothing voice.

He was surprised that she'd actually shown up in fatigues. For some reason, he couldn't get his head around the fact that she was an officer in the Army. He could only see her as a doctor.

Over the years, he had seen many a woman in fatigues, but not a one that had made them look feminine...not until Dylan. The formless outfit had begged to hug her curves.

Holden cursed himself for looking at her body. All he wanted was to get to know this woman who had loved his brother. Nothing else.

"Looking for company?" Accompanied her knock on the door.

Tamping down his excitement, he watched her walk into the room. She was in the same outfit as she had been in the day before, the caduceus on display for all to know she was into medicine.

"Yes, I am. Sorry I fell asleep on you," he said as she briskly walked to the bed.

"Medication will do that. Or my boring stories." She pulled on a pair of gloves she had grabbed from a box near the door.

"It's the medication; your stories are great." He watched her check and redress his leg again.

Watching her pull the blue gloves off and ball them into her hand, he noticed something on her wrist. Sitting up, he grabbed it and looked at it. He noticed the large caduceus on her left arm whenever he saw her, but never the small tattoo on her right arm. Running up her blue vain was his last name written in fancy cursive.

"It's a copy of his signature," she whispered and gently pulled her arm from his grasp.

"Why didn't you just show me this when I was being an ass, saying you weren't mourning enough?" he demanded, feeling like the heel he was that day.

Her hand covered the entire tattoo as she answered, "Because I don't have to prove I loved him, not to anyone. He knew, and that's all that mattered."

With effort, he swung his legs off the bed and took two careful steps toward her. Without a word, he put his arms around her and hugged her as tight as he could. Her body was as solid as he thought it was going to be, solid and soft all at the same time.

At his first touch, she had stiffened, but her stance had softened instantly as he held her tight. In his arms, she wasn't a small woman, she was tall and willowy.

Bending his head so that he was near her ear, he whispered, "I'm sorry I ever said anything to hurt you, Dylan. My brother couldn't have found someone better, and I'm a little jealous. Nobody has *my* name tattooed on them."

"You've obviously been dating the wrong women." Her hands slid around him, and he hoped it wasn't because she thought he would fall down and she would need to hold him up.

"Oh? And where's my Dylan, then?" He wanted the words back as soon as he said them. There was no understanding, loving woman for him—he was a lone wolf and always would be.

"Out there somewhere," she said, but he was too busy thinking out this one. There seemed to be only one Dylan, and his brother had claimed her long ago.

"Can you get back to the bed?" she asked.

"Yes, Doc, I can. I've been practicing all day, so I can get out of here by tomorrow." He reluctantly dropped his arms from around her, letting her take a step away from him.

Looking into her blue eyes, he wondered if she felt the same sparks that were racing through his body. Or was he alone and going insane?

Slowly, he walked back to the bed and sat down with a flourish, just to prove he could.

"Good job." She sounded like a parent with a three-year-old. "But you need to be more mobile if you expect them to let you out tomorrow."

They weren't talking about the hug or the words he'd said. She was back to being the doctor, a position she was comfortable with.

"They're thinking of putting me up in that swanky place you live in, Doc, at least for a week or so. Less sand." He had been told this morning, now he wished he had seen the inside of her room because he had no idea what he was getting into. From the rumor he'd heard, it was like a prison, with small rooms and no comfort.

"That is what the ground floor is for," she said, leaning against the cabinets again.

"Maybe I'll see you in the bathroom, then." He grinned at her.

"Nope, those are still separate. Probably won't see me at all." She rarely saw anyone around the building. Most people kept to themselves.

"When I get my strength up, I can come to your room, and we can have these conversations at your place."

"I don't know how much more you want to know, Captain. It was a long time ago," she reminded him.

"Did Chase want kids?" His brother had died so young, were kids even on his radar? After all these years, both his other brothers had them now; he was the last holdout.

"Not with me." Her hands gripped the countertop, turning her knuckles white.

"Because you didn't want any or because he didn't want any?" he asked since her answer didn't seem right. Not after yesterday's talk of the love and devotion that they had.

"I didn't want kids; I knew that even then. It was something we were still talking about, but only because he wasn't going to change my mind."

"Because you can't?"

"Because I won't. I was raised in an abusive home. I carry the gene; I'm not abusing my children."

"It's not a gene, Dylan."

"Whatever it is, I am prone to it." She actually looked at her hands, the hands that had saved lives day after day for years, as if they would betray her.

"I don't see it," he said, looking at her hands also.

"Ask me about Marquez, not about me, please," she stated calmly, shoving her hands in her pockets.

"What was his argument with you about your gene? I bet he didn't believe you either," he asked her, noticing anger in her blue eyes.

"That was between us, not you." She folded her arms across her chest in defense. With a sigh, she headed for the door as she said, "Good luck, Captain, and watch out for those bullets. Next time, you might not be so lucky."

"Stay," he said from his bed, know she was leaving and not coming back.

"I have things I need to do before work tomorrow." She didn't turn back to him.

"Can I at least hug you goodbye?" he asked, his arms were still tingling from when he had held her tight the first time.

"No, Holden. Get well soon." She was out the door before he could stop her. Out the door and out of his life. He had pushed too far, and she had bolted. As usual, he'd let his mouth get in the way.

CHAPTER 9

"And then Ryan dumps the fish tank over my sister Kim's head. Thank God it wasn't Todd's mother." Elissa had tears running down her face as she told the story about her kid's antics. It was a wonder the man let her leave him alone with the beasts, and there were only two of them.

"At least the fish was already dead." Dylan grinned at her friend.

Elissa was laughing again. "Can you imagine the fish in all that?"

"I'm glad everyone is still in good spirits; only a few more weeks for you." Dylan tried to not let it hurt that she was losing a friend…again.

No matter where she was, stateside or here, people were always coming and going. Staff was never static. When Elissa left, someone would be there to replace her—probably not as fun, but hopefully just as competent because more important than a friend, she needed staff she could count on.

Elissa was again leaning against her desk. This time, it was mid-shift, and the OR had settled down. They didn't get a lot of overnight injuries; more happened in the morning than any at other time of the day.

"A little bird told me you were here for a visit with a patient during your time off." Elissa was reading a folder on a soldier who was being sent home in the a.m.. Head injury.

"It isn't what you think," Dylan told her. She didn't want Elissa thinking it was about sex.

"I think you like him, which is perfectly fine. I mean, he *is* an amazing hunk of a man. I can only imagine what he's like between the sheets." Elissa didn't look up from her folder.

"You are getting way too much phone sex, my friend, so get your mind out of the gutter. We happen to have a mutual friend, and he was asking me questions about that person."

"Was it me? Did you tell him I was married? It probably broke his heart. Did you pick up the pieces? Tell him how free you are. I mean, second choice isn't all that bad." Elissa snapped the folder shut with a chuckle.

"Always about you. But anyway, he's been discharged and is gone. I hope he takes care of his leg." She tried to concentrate on her paperwork—even on a slow shift, there was a lot of it.

"Two days' worth of talking?" Elissa kept probing.

"One day of talking. The other was a waste of time. We don't really get along," she admitted. There was too much of a past between them, even if they had spent more time together now than ever.

"Doesn't mean you can't have some fun. I mean, you can fuck him without liking him, right?" Elissa, Ms. I've only slept with one guy, asked innocently.

"I am not sleeping with him," she stated sternly.

"Come on, Dyl, how is he any different from the other guys? Dr. Narcissist? You slept with him. And that sniveling corporal with the bad teeth? You did him. But this guy, who even I think is hot, is off limits?" Elissa argued.

"Due to our mutual friend."

"Is your mutual friend going to get pissed? Hate you both forever? Call out a vendetta against you?" Elissa read too much, and her taste in books leaned toward the mafia. Sometimes, it showed.

"He's dead."

"See, no hurt feelings. Just do what you want—the dead guy will never now."

"But I'll know," she reminded her friend.

"And you also want him. I can tell when you want something, and you want him. You don't visit patients, and never three times. What is it about this guy? Unless you saw his weewee?" She grinned.

"You would think that after nearly a year here, you would start using actual terms for body parts."

"Fine, his *cock*, Dr. Smarty Pants," she said as both their phones chimed at once. Without a word, both left the office and the fun behind —it was time to work.

A couple of hours and two surgeries later, Dylan finally headed home to her barracks room that had no personality and no real comfort. Her shift had ended up running long again, and she was feeling it. Once the adrenaline had worn off, she was exhausted.

Heading toward the stairs, she suddenly heard her name being called. Turning, she saw Holden leaning against an open door frame, as if he were waiting for her. *What? There's no way he could have known I was coming home now.*

"Captain." She stopped and turned to him. He was back in fatigues topped with an Army T-shirt that matched hers, but his molded to his broad chest and arms. He didn't look gray or white, he looked normal. Like he hadn't been shot a few days before.

"Didn't think I would see you around here," he said casually.

She pointed up. "Just got off shift. Heading home."

"And you have to pass my room to get there." He grinned as he jerked his chin toward the room behind him.

"I guess I do. Hope you're enjoying the warm, comfortable accommodations." She looked past him at the sparse room beyond.

"It's definitely more like a prison than a home, but with much less sand than I'm used to."

"We still get the desert creatures, though, so watch out," she warned and turned to get home. As uncomfortable as it was, her bed was calling to her.

"Can we talk for a moment?" His words stopped her.

"We don't talk well, Captain."

"It's Holden, and just for a minute." He gestured for her to enter his room.

Rolling her eyes at the idea, she went anyway; sleep could wait a minute or two. His room seemed immediately different than hers. His manly woodsy smell, even here in the desert, was everywhere.

"Sit." She gestured at the bed. Coming out of surgery, nobody was as strong as they liked to think they were.

"You first," he challenged her.

Hesitantly, she sat on the bed, knowing he would have to fix it when she left. The bed was just like hers, made in the exact same way. *Oh, the Army life.*

"Okay, fine. I'm sitting," she stated and watched him sit on the other end. He sighed as he lowered himself down on the bed. He wasn't even close to 100% yet.

"I just wanted to say I'm sorry I pushed you. Your stuff is your stuff. I'll try not to do it again. Next time, just tell me to shut up—maybe I'll take the hint." He grinned at her because they both knew he would pry, and she would get mad.

"I'll accept your apology, but only because I'm tired and have no fight in me right now," she admitted.

"A weak moment? Doc Dylan had a weak moment?" he asked her playfully.

"Happens to the best of us, Captain."

"It's Holden, and I think I'll take advantage of your weak moment," he said with a wink, then grabbed her shoulders and started massaging them.

"I should get home," she murmured, not getting up because then he would stop.

"You're a tense woman, you know? How about as an apology, I give you a massage and then send you to bed? It'll be the most relaxing sleep you will get while here." His hands didn't stop, but somehow guided her so she was face-down on his bed, purring in contentment.

Holden was sending wave after wave of heat through her body, and with his smell surrounding her, she surrendered to the amazing things his hands were doing. Soon, exhaustion finally won out, and she fell asleep on his bed.

CHAPTER 10

HOLDEN KNEW the moment she fell sleep, as all the tension in her body vanished. It wasn't gradual; it was simply there, then gone. He kept rubbing her back and shoulders anyway because he couldn't stop himself.

He didn't know if she was having a particularly rough shift, but today, she was stressed. The exhaustion had her guard down though, leading her to his room instead of fighting him.

He decided to let her sleep for a while, forcing his hands to stop touching her. He wasn't using his bed, anyway. After unlacing her boots and pulling them off, he found an extra blanket and draped it over her body. Even in the climate-controlled building, there was no way to keep all the heat out, but he felt better with her under the blanket.

Sitting in the lone, uncomfortable chair, he watched her sleep for a while. Her loose brown hair tumbled around her, still slightly damp. He realized she must shower at the hospital before coming home to sleep. As his mind went instantly to her naked in the shower, she groaned in her sleep and rolled onto her side, facing away from him. The blanket moved slightly, and he got up and fixed it so that it was covering her more. Not at all because it gave him an excuse to touch her shoulder or her hair.

He was turning into a pervert for this one woman, the one woman he couldn't have. He knew that, even if his dick wasn't on the same page as him.

Eyeing the chair, he wanted to sit and watch her more, making sure she stayed comfortable, but he forced himself out of the room. He didn't know how long she would sleep, but he was sure it was going to be hours.

The sun had set by the time he finally let himself back into his room. He fully expected her to be gone, to have roused enough over the past few hours to go to her room. But she was still in his bed, almost exactly where he had left her, except her head was now snuggled into his pillow, and the blanket was on the floor.

On the floor were also her camo pants and socks. Quietly, he went over and picked them up, folding them and placing them on his dresser. All the while trying to ignore that she was sleeping in his bed in only her T-shirt and red lace panties. Not a distraction *at all*.

Picking up the blanket, he began folding it as another scrap of clothing tumbled to the floor. Somehow, she had done the lady magic thing of taking off her bra, but not her shirt. *Had she done that in her sleep?*

"Dyl, it's time to get up." He shook her shoulder lightly because if he picked any other location on her gorgeous body, his hand would stray.

Her only answer was a mumble about it being hot, and she rolled away from him. Trying again, he shook her shoulder and said her name again. This time, she opened her eyes and sat up. Dylan said nothing as she looked around his room.

"Time to go home," he said again as she looked right at him, then fell back into the pillow behind her—sound asleep.

Clearly, there was no waking her. Her body needed sleep, and it was getting it no matter what, so he sat down again. For the next hour, she didn't move; not a hair, not anything. He knew that he couldn't sleep in a chair; he was exhausted himself.

He could sleep on the floor, which was concrete and didn't even have a carpet over it, or sleep with her. Based on her state, she wasn't getting up anytime soon.

His two options were to go to her room and sleep in her bed or crawl in with her in his. But he wouldn't getting any sleep with her inches from him. He was already having a hard time keeping his hands to himself.

He found her keys in the pocket of her pants. They were on a keychain made by some kid from Picard string in red, white, and blue. He was sure it had been sent in a care package she randomly received at some point from a school sending stuff to soldiers. Holden smiled as he left the room, knowing that a kid somewhere in the States had no idea his or her soldier was still using the keychain they'd made.

Holden climbed up three flights of stairs and unlocked her door, then left it ajar as he brought the keys back to her and put them back in her pocket. If she thought they were gone, she might not just head home, but start looking for them.

Back up the stairs, he let himself into her room, a carbon copy of his. In fact, she had little that distinguished the room she had been in for almost two years from the one he had been in for two days. The desk had a pile of papers and there was an e-reader plugged in on it, all perfectly straight. He couldn't see any pictures or letters.

Without stopping himself, he opened the two desk drawers. Both were empty, save for a couple of pens.

Dresser drawers were just perfect stacks of clothing; straight lines and order. The closet was the same, except for a shoe box on the top shelf. The box had been smashed a few times, making it seem out of place.

He wanted to see if she had anything of Chase's in the box, so he pulled it off the shelf. It was full of letters. Looking at the return addresses, some had a kid's handwriting on them, and some had been sent from Minneapolis.

Holden chose a letter at random and picked it up. It was from someone named Janet Dylannski Reed and had been sent seven years before. It was unopened, as were almost all the letters, all still sealed shut by whoever cared enough to send her a letter. All the letters from Janet were addressed to Jessica Dylannski. Not a one had Marquez on it or Doctor or Major, just her name. Except one, the one that said Jess.

It suddenly hit him that she was still estranged from her family, but that they wanted her back. He wondered what had happened to keep her away from them for twenty years, but they still wrote, a lot. Would someone who abused her really keep writing?

After putting the box back on the shelf, he shed his clothes because it was even hotter up on the higher floors. Down to his boxers, he slid into her bed and rolled onto his side. He looked at her clean bedside table and thought, *She keeps herself distant from everything*. All she had was her work, and she was pushing herself too hard with that. What happened if she broke?

He must have fallen asleep instantly, because the next thing he knew, the door to the room opened. It was still dark, and she didn't turn on the light when she came in.

He knew he should've said something, but when her pants hit the ground, he was speechless. All he could do was watch as she folded them and put them in the drawer with the other ones just like it. Then she tossed the socks and bra she was carrying in a laundry bag.

She was getting ready for bed just by the light of the moon. The same moon that was giving him a show he shouldn't be watching. Shouldn't be enjoying.

As she grabbed the hem of her T-shirt, he finally cleared his throat, letting her know he was there. Her stifled scream ended in a curse.

"What are you *doing* here?" she demanded of him.

"I was tired, and you weren't getting up, so I left you down there." He wondered if his explanation made sense to her.

"Well, I'm up now, so you can have your bed back."

"Okay, but I'm only in my boxers," he warned her with a grin.

"And I'm not nearly naked?" she bit back.

"It's little different for you, Doc, your body doesn't announce what it's thinking." He talked around it, though it was painful as he looked at her bare legs in the moonlight.

"You have a hard-on? Get over yourself, Holden. I've seen plenty of them over the years." She shook her head, sending her hair swirling around her.

"I like to think mine is special."

She raised a brow at him. "All guys do. So, either you leave my bed or make room. I have four more hours of sleep before my run."

"I came up here to *not* sleep with you." He swung his legs over the side of the bed, hard-on be damned. She didn't care, anyway.

"Nothing you have interests me." Despite what she said, her eyes went south for a long second.

"Nothing?" he questioned as he got to his feet and walked up to her. The corner of his mouth pulling up in a mischievous smile.

"Nope, not a thing." Her fingers were still on the hem of her shirt, fiddling with it now.

With a finger, he traced her jawline. "I think you're lying, Dylan."

"I am not," she sputtered but stayed frozen to the spot.

Looking into her dark eyes in the moonlight, he ran his fingers down her arms to her hands, taking each one in his as he brought them to his lips and kissed them lightly. Then he brought them back to her sides. He let her go for a moment, then his hands slid around her waist.

With their eyes still locked, he grabbed the hem of her shirt and started pulling it up, ever so slowly, watching for signs she didn't want this. None came when the shirt broke their eye contact as he lifted it over her head.

Her fingertips brushed his chest, and the light touch had him groaning her name. Dragging her into him, his mouth caught hers in a soul-draining kiss. As their lips and tongues battled for control, their hands were everywhere at once. All the fighting they had done since the beginning was now focused on this.

Holden moved across the small room until the backs of his knees hit the bed, and in one fluid motion, he took her down with him. His eyes avoided the necklace with the gold band on it, focusing more on the breasts around it. He guided her onto his lap so that she straddled him, but the bullet wound got in the way, so he lifted her off with a growl and rolled her underneath him. The new position allowed him to gaze at her firm breasts as she heaved for breath, letting him just look.

With a grin, he took a nipple in his mouth and reveled in the feel of it, the perfectness of the moment. He wanted to take it slow and savor every moment of this. But she had other ideas.

Without him noticing, she had slid out of her panties and was making fast work of his boxers. After running his hands over her breasts and stomach, he headed lower, only to have her grab them and pull them away from her core.

"No need for that, I'm wet already," she whispered as she rolled him onto his back. She was in control now.

Within seconds, she had slipped a condom on him and had slid her tight little body onto his shaft. Groaning at the sensation of being encased in her, he wished they had all the time in the world.

Her hands went to her hair as she increased the tempo until she was moaning. Before he could get his hands on her perfect, full breasts, an orgasm exploded through her, which had her squeezing his cock, bringing him to an early climax.

And just like that, it was over. He lay there panting as she climbed off him. With energy he didn't possess, he sat up and took off the condom, tossing it in her trash. He rolled over and gathered her in his arms, but she pushed him away, mumbling about how hot she was.

Once again, he knew she had fallen asleep because of how her body finally relaxed. He looked at her as she lay in the moonlight, her hair a mess and her body covered in a delicate sheen of sweat.

They had just had sex, and she had treated it like everything else in her life: with order and regiment. He could've been anyone with a cock for all she cared—it wasn't about him; it was about her getting off. What he wanted didn't matter, only that she got what she needed from him.

Knowing he wouldn't sleep after that, he got up, not carrying if he woke her this time. Holden watched her as he pulled on his clothes, but she didn't move despite him making as much noise as he could. Her bare back was all he saw when he looked at her. He could see faint lines running across the creamy white skin. Though faint, somehow, he knew they were scars from a belt.

Sitting on the edge of her bed, he brushed his hand gently over them. There were dozens of them. There was so much she didn't, wouldn't, talk about with him. Probably with anyone.

As he got up, Holden realized he wanted more from her than just sex. He wanted to know her and understand what made her the way she was. Maybe even show her that she could enjoy life…if she let him.

CHAPTER 11

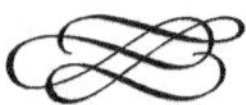

AVOIDING Holden Marquez had turned into a game—a game she was pretty good at. Or maybe he wasn't looking for her, making it only seem like she was good at the game, when there was actually no game at all.

It had been two weeks since they had sex, and she knew he was back with his unit; back where he belonged. More importantly, he was not in a room on her way to the stairs. As hard as she tried not to, her eyes also looked at his old door on the way by, even though she knew he was long gone.

Sitting in her office in the middle of the day, she finally had a moment to herself. She had the door shut and the lights off, trying to meditate—though she had never done it before, so she had no idea what she should be doing. Instead, sex with Holden was playing over and over in her mind.

Sex was probably why he had left that night, or more likely, not wanting to have sex with her again. There was no way she could ever kid herself into thinking he had enjoyed it; she hadn't enjoyed it all that much herself.

Wishing she could go back and let him lead the way wasn't going to help, so she pushed all thoughts of him back into the pit of the past where they belonged. She didn't need his approval or his admiration. She was her own person, and she made her own rules.

Light from the hallway suddenly blared into the room, causing her to squint. Elissa pushed her way into the room with a smile. Shut doors meant nothing to the bubbly woman.

"Got a headache, Dyl?" she asked in concern.

"No, just relaxing," she told her friend who was always concerned about her health.

"Oh, sorry! I just have a few reports for you to sign, then I'll leave you alone." She shoved the files into Dylan's hands as she turned on the office lights.

"Okay." Dylan sighed and started scribbling her signature on all the papers that needed it. The shaking had lessened while she had been in the dark, but it wasn't gone completely.

"Maybe you should just call him. I can get his number." Elissa watched her hand.

"I don't need to call him. It was a one-time thing." Another document was signed and she immediately regretted telling Elissa anything. But the woman had a way of getting her to tell all her secrets. Or some of them, at least.

"You've been more on edge since it happened, and you're already on edge all the time as it is! I have knives duller than you, Dylan," Elissa said in exasperation.

"Thanks, I sound like a pleasant person." Dylan handed all the folders back to her.

"You are, Dyl, one of my favorites. But you *are* unique," Elissa pressed carefully.

"I would take that as a compliment, but I don't really think it is."

"It was, it definitely was. Now I have a surprise for you." Elissa hugged the folders to her, eyes twinkling.

"What?" Dylan hated surprises, there were never happy ones.

"I *might* have called him." She slapped her hand to her mouth, covering a smile.

"Who?"

She was still covering her mouth as she said, "Holden."

"Why!?" she demanded, hating how her heart was fluttering at the mere mention of his name.

"Because that's what friends do. You would do the same for me." She started backing from the room, still grinning at Dylan.

"Just call him back and tell him it was a mistake!" she yelled after the woman who was already out the door.

His handsome, smiling face then leaned over and looked at her through the open door, saying, "I'll just pretend I didn't hear that."

Scrubbing her hands over her face, she cursed under her breath. She wished seeing him didn't make her happy and that she could ignore the flip-flop of her heart.

"Missed you too, Dylan." Holden calmly walked into the room. He was in full fatigues today and was completely covered in sand, even around his smile and dark eyes. She had to admit he made a dirty soldier look good.

"Captain," she responded professionally, hoping she kept every ounce of excitement out of her voice.

"It's Holden. I wanted to see you." He sat in the lone visitor chair in her office, his presence taking over the entire room.

"I'm working right now." She lifted her hands and gestured vaguely around her office, still not turning to look at him completely.

"I needed to see you, Dylan. I can't stop thinking about you." His voice suddenly took on a more serious note.

"Elissa called you," she reminded him.

"Her call just had me coming before showering and getting pretty for you." He grabbed her knee and spun her in her chair toward him.

"Quit flirting, Captain." She looked at his hand on her knee. Her heart picked up its already quickened pace.

Holden just looked at her for moment before saying, "I've decided that what you need is a little romance in your life." He pulled her chair closer to his by her leg, and damn if that chair didn't just slide right up to him.

"The *last* thing I need is romance," she argued, but her voice faltered just a little.

"I can't *not* romance you, Dylan. Everything inside me tells me you need this. All of it." His hand slid up her knee, then up her side, around her shoulder, and behind her neck.

She let it happen, and truthfully, she wanted what he was planning. To her surprise, he leaned into her as he pulled her even closer toward him. His lips brushed against hers ever so lightly, just a touch and a warm breath against her closed mouth. Then it was gone.

Sitting back, he smiled at her as if he knew he'd knocked her completely off kilter. Leaning away from her again, he returned his hand on her knee.

"When are you done here today?" he asked as his thumb made a lazy circle over her inner thigh.

"Tomorrow morning." Every one of her nerves was pinpointed to her thigh as she watched his hand instead of his face.

"Then you'll sleep?"

Her breath stopped as his hand slowly inched upward. "Yes."

"I'll come and get you tomorrow later in the day and take you to eat. Whatever meal it happens to be." His hand stopped just short of the seam of her scrubs.

"No," she whispered, wondering if it was in response to his offer or because his hand had stopped.

With a slow smile, he leaned forward again, and she could feel his breath on her ear when he whispered, "Yes."

A shiver ran down her spine at that one word, with all its promise and threat. Closing her eyes, she enjoyed the sensations washing over her.

The annoying chime on her phone had her on her feet before she could warn him of what it was. Picking the thing off her desk, she read where she was needed, then turned to him. She didn't actually know what to say. Did she explain what was happening? Could he guess?

"Go, Dylan. See you tomorrow." He didn't get up, only smiled at her. He didn't need her to explain her job to him.

Out the door without a word, she headed to the OR. Elissa would be there almost as soon as Dylan would. They were in the same OR this week.

Pulling on the protective material over her scrubs, she hoped that her hands wouldn't fail her today. It was getting worse over the last couple of months, not better, and nothing she had tried had helped yet. She knew she was losing her edge when Elissa offered to help her tie the back of her scrubs for her.

CHAPTER 12

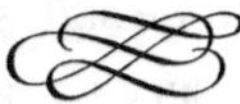

ROMANCING the doctor had become the only thing he could think of. If he wasn't on a mission, he was coming up with ways to woo the amazing, prickly woman in the middle of a war zone.

Flowers were obviously not happening. Such an easy thing back in the States was impossible in the desert. Instead, he had drawn her a picture of them and left them on her desk. After hours of fighting for someone's life, she would come back to them.

Next, he had mailed a letter containing another drawing of different flowers, knowing she would get them when she picked up her mail after work. He wished he could see her face when she saw either one—would she just think he was cheesy?

Dylan had been right that it had taken Elissa's call to kick him in the pants about the doctor. In the two weeks since he had left her bed, he had thought about her nonstop, but not enough to talk to her.

But Elissa had changed that with her matter-of-factness about the small part of Dylan's life that she knew. That she was a loner, to the point that she never got letters, ever. Not from family, friends, or old colleagues; all relationships were short-term in her life, and most sexual ones ended after the first date. She never went for a man who pursued her—she *always* pursued them.

Sadly, the woman had said nothing Holden hadn't already known from talking to her...and from snooping in her room. Elissa didn't know about the letters she got from her family; the ones she'd left unopened.

What Elissa did tell him was that Dylan was burning out. It was taking everything out of her to keep up the pace she was at, and she was starting to fail. Elissa was concerned that if Dylan didn't find an outlet for her tension, she would be stateside soon.

After almost two years of serving in the desert, burnout was a distinct possibility; even he could tell she was nothing but a working machine. No one could live their life that way without burning out in the end, which was why he was redoubling his effort to get her to relax and enjoy herself. He would do it for his brother, not for himself. Even if it seemed she was trying to kill herself.

Knocking on her door, he hoped he had given her enough time to sleep; she clearly needed it. He began to worry that she was avoiding him again when he had to knock a second time. When she finally opened the door, her dark hair was still wet, and her feet were bare.

"I didn't think you would be this early," she said as she turned away from him to grab a perfectly folded pair of socks from her dresser.

"Sorry, I didn't give you a time." He stepped in and watched as she pulled on the socks and then her boots.

While she was looking away, he pulled out the three chocolate candy bars he had purchased on the way over and set them on her dresser in a neat pile. It wasn't quite what bringing candy to your lover looked like, but it was as close as he was going to get. Sadly, they were already partially melted and would be worse after spending a few hours in this room. Her eyes watched him, but she didn't comment about it.

He wasn't sure if he had thought she'd wear something other than fatigues to dinner, but then again, he knew she didn't have anything else. Her damp hair hid her face as she tied the laces on her boots.

"Did you sleep well?" he asked when she sat up and ran her fingers through her hair to push it off her face.

"Usually," she answered as she grabbed a shirt from the closet and slid it over her T-shirt.

"Is usual good or bad?"

"Like the dead for hours, and then more fitfully. Have you been out since I saw you?" She finished buttoning the shirt, leaving him missing the form-fitting T-shirt.

"Yeah, this morning. It went well." He didn't go into it; there was nothing that made it exciting or interesting. Nothing like watching her fingers braid her thick hair, which *was* interesting.

"Well, that's good." She tied it off and added her hat before adding, "Ready."

Grinning, he stepped close to her, and with his thumb, touched her pink lip before trailing it down to her chin, raising it so he could brush a light kiss over her mouth. He fought the urge to deepen it, to kiss her like he wanted to. Instead, he rained kisses over her face and to her ear where he whispered, "You look beautiful today, Dylan."

"I didn't try to," she sighed and let him kiss her again.

"You don't have to." His lips brushed hers again, and though she leaned into it, he pulled away. This wasn't about sex; this was about him showing her that there was more to a relationship than sex.

Without another word, he took her hand in his and led her from the room and out of the building. He was half-surprised that she went willingly and didn't even say anything about holding his hand in public.

Three hours later, after a hot walk around the hospital, they were still hand in hand. They talked over supper at the canteen, mostly about nothing—Dylan didn't talk about herself easily. And now that they were "dating," they didn't talk about his brother. When Holden had brought him up, she had shut down the conversation quickly.

Now he had her back pressed against her door and was kissing her neck. Though his hands were on the wall above her head, she didn't move away from him. In fact, she was giving him every signal to move their "conversation" to the bedroom. And as much as he wanted that, he had a mission to accomplish with her.

Moving from her neck and across her chin to her lips, he felt rather than heard her murmurs of approval. As her hands ran up his chest, he finally deepened the kiss, letting her have her way. His tongue met hers when her fingers dug into his shirt, pulling him even closer to her.

Reluctantly, he pulled back, letting out a long sigh. He wanted everything she was offering, but he wasn't going to let her be in charge this time. They were taking it slow, and if he went into that room, there would be nothing slow about what happened next.

"Are you free tomorrow?" He kissed her forehead.

"I'm off, yeah."

"Do you want to do this again?"

She looked up at him and smirked. "Are you going to leave me high and dry again?"

"Probably. I want you to *want* me in your bed." He flashed his mischievous smile at her.

"Don't worry, I want you there pretty bad right now." She tried to pull him close to her.

"Me, as in Holden? Or just some cock with no name?" He watched anger overtake her at his words.

"Are you calling me a whore?" she demanded, now pushing him away.

"What? No, Dylan, but I want to be more than a cock for you to ride whenever you have the urge." He kept her caged against the wall, not letting her storm away from him like she usually did.

"I think we *both* enjoyed that," she spat out.

He tried to soothe her by softening his tone. "Getting off and enjoying are two different things. I want to enjoy my time with you, not just get off."

"I thought you wanted to romance me?" she said in a mocking voice.

"I want you to see that having an orgasm isn't all there is to sex. I want you looking into my eyes as you come and have you screaming my name. Because you know it." He let her push him away this time. She could have her way…for now.

"Aren't you old enough to know that sex is just sex, Captain? That foreplay is just the fluff you don't need?" She stopped at her door and shot back at him.

"When you're ready to for actual sex, Dylan, I'm going to fluff the hell out of you. And you'll be begging for more." He watched her roll her eyes at him and close her door behind her.

It wasn't exactly the ending to the great night he was looking for, but now she knew the rules. And now, he was more excited to "fluff" with her than anything he had done in a long time.

～

"So, you've been dating this guy for three weeks now, and I'm having more sex than you even though my man is on the other side of the planet?" Elissa stated in disbelief.

Sadly, it was true. Every day she had off, he was there for a date, which included him bringing gifts and them sharing a meal at the canteen, which was the most unromantic place ever created.

The gifts ranged from semi-melted candy bars to socks, which is what he gave her on their last date. Oddly, they were actual socks, not Army-issued ones. Dylan was seeing that he was running out of things to give her but wasn't giving up on the "romance her to death" part of their dating.

And all she really wanted was a good old-fashioned roll in the hay. Okay, not too old-fashioned, because she was horny as hell. Every date ended with him kissing her until she was panting and wanting more. Then he would walk away, leaving her frustrated.

In reality, she should just stop with the dating thing; it was weird. She was almost forty, beyond the dating scene, but for some reason, she got excited and couldn't not go out with him.

The fact that he was Marquez's brother rarely crossed her mind anymore. Maybe it was because he was older than her husband had ever been or that they didn't resemble each other very much. Or, she hated to admit, that maybe it was because she was ready to move on with her life, and that her young love was a long time ago.

"I guess we're taking it slowly," Dylan said as she tried to concentrate on the chart in front of her, or more importantly, ignore Elissa.

"Did you tell him this a war zone? You can't take it slowly!" Elissa sounded as frustrated as she felt.

"Nope, since he's actually seeing the war, I thought it would be rude." She closed the file to give her friend her full attention.

"Did you ask to see his battle scars?" Elissa said, straight-faced.

"You mean the one six inches from his penis?" she asked, wondering if it would work.

"I thought it was seven?" Elissa grinned at her, knowing it was closer than either of them guessed.

"No, I haven't, even though I have a professional interest in how it's healing."

"You do! I mean, you have to make sure the stitches healed properly. And what about infection? You shouldn't be taking chances on that." Elissa cracked a smile.

"I think six weeks is maybe too long to be requesting a look-see." And that was actually her professional opinion.

"Should we make a bet that I have sex again before you? And I have to spend three more weeks here, then fly for twenty-four hours to get it," Elissa complained, as if another day of waiting would kill her.

"I don't need a countdown calendar like you sent Todd. If it happens, it happens. If not, oh well." She shrugged.

"Don't 'oh well' me. You are a horny woman. You need to just tackle that man, unless…" Elissa eyed her closely, too closely.

"What?" she demanded.

"You're *enjoying* the romance! His corny gifts and make-out sessions are working!" Elissa danced with excitement.

"I am not," she argued, but it was true, she was loving it. But who wouldn't love a guy who gave her one of his shirts to sleep in so she'd think of him? And she had a notebook full of pictures of flowers, drawn in black pen that had no color to them at all. He mailed them all the time.

"Liar, liar, pants on fire. I love it, Dr. No Commitment is falling for this guy."

"Not falling, just enjoying it, okay!"

"What's the worst thing that could happen if you actually fell for him? I think you two are cute together."

Dylan gave her a flat stare. "I'm like a decade older than him."

"Who cares? He doesn't."

"I am never stateside."

"But you could be; you've put in your time. And you can come back when he does. You could make it work. Others do."

"His parents hate me," she countered. It was an obstacle they wouldn't overcome.

"How would you know? Do you know his parents? Did you know him before?" Elissa stopped pacing and looked at her intently.

"Whoops." She rubbed her face with her hands. Six weeks had gone by, and she hadn't told her friend the truth.

"Whoops, what?" Elissa pulled her hands off her face.

"Holden is Chase's younger brother. His parents hated me when we were married."

"You slept with your husband's brother?" Elissa's eyes were huge as she asked.

"I told you we aren't sleeping together," she said lamely. Was she actually whining?

"Yeah, except for that first time. Holy cow, his brother. Are they alike? In the sack, I mean?" Elissa leaned closer to her, eyebrows shooting higher with every question.

"Oddly, they're completely different. Or maybe it's that Holden grew up and Marquez never got to. I usually don't remember they're brothers," she admitted

"So, you knew him? All this time, and you never told me?" Elissa demanded.

"He was sixteen when Marquez died, and I was not invited to anything but the burial. At the time, I wasn't exactly scoping out the guys there."

"You're right, you're right. I couldn't date Todd's brother, though. He's an ass."

"Don't date him then," Dylan stated, smirking.

Elissa gave her the finger. "Why didn't Mr. Marquez's parents like you?"

"Because my magic pussy kept their son from going home after basic training." She winked at her.

"Ohhh, and now the magic pussy might lead another astray." Elissa giggled.

"No, this is just fun for now. One of us will get transferred, and then it'll be over. There's no future."

"Blah, blah, blah. There's no future because *you* don't want one. He's proven that you can't control him, and you hate that."

"I like a little bit of organization in my life! Chaos is not enjoyable."

"Yes, it is. All you have to do is let loose a little. Chaos is the spice of life."

"I thought the spice of life was variety?"

"Variety is just another word for chaos."

"Completely different," she argued as they headed out for the day. Their shift was over, and it was time for a few hours of sleep before another date with Holden. She didn't want to admit that she was really looking forward to it.

Elissa stopped off and grabbed something to eat at the canteen, letting Dylan walk alone back to the barracks. It was already hot, and the sun had barely risen. She knew Holden was out on a mission today, and she hoped he was okay. She hated that his job was dangerous, but he was a soldier.

Inside the semi-cooled building, she stopped and grabbed her mail, something she had grown to enjoy since Holden had started mailing her little things all the time. Every day she got a letter, nothing big or great, but a little something to remind her he was thinking of her.

Opening the box, she pulled out three envelopes: two from Holden since she had worked for twenty-four hours, and one from Janet. Flipping it to the back of the pile, she opened Holden's letter from the day before. It was a thinking of you card, written on plan notebook paper. Nothing fancy, but it made her smile. Opening the next one, she saw it was a long, lengthy letter. Shoving it back in the envelope, she cursed herself—she had opened Janet's letter by mistake.

After twenty years, she still didn't open those, it didn't matter how many Janet sent. What happened was in the past, and there was nothing the woman could say to make it all better.

Janet had chosen which of her children she was going to love long before Dylan then, but she had proved what she really thought of her firstborn that year. It still churned her stomach to think about those days.

Janet had always known that Jesse was abusive; she had left him because of it just a few years before. For years, the woman had hidden behind the facade of being a perfect corporate wife by not showing the world the bruises that Jesse caused to her and their two children.

But still, she was willing to send a seventeen-year-old to live full time with the man again. To face beating after beating, all because of Janet's precious Jenna had told her sister was hitting her.

Janet herself would never lift a hand against her own children, but she allowed someone else to. She even dropped Dylan off for it and left her there.

Dylan had spent four months in the hell that was her father's house; four months of abuse. Her only option had been to run off and join the Army—her mother was done with her, and Dylan couldn't take it anymore.

How Janet had found out she had joined up, she didn't know, but the woman was persistent. Every month or so, she sent another letter. Was she apologizing? Was she asking her to come home? Dylan had no idea because she never, ever read them, even though she couldn't bring herself to throw them out. She even carried the box across the world with her.

Janet almost always had Dylan's correct mailing address, so she must have been calling to get that information. When her father had died three years after Marquez, her CO had talked to her mother and told Janet that Dylan would not be going home for the funeral. At the time, she was on her first tour in Iraq, and she didn't need to see that man dead. He was already dead to her years before.

Her CO had told her that her mom had cried and begged for information about her daughter, but it was all classified. Thankfully, he hadn't told the woman her new name, that she had been married, or even what she was doing in the Army. Dylan was sure her mom thought she was just a soldier.

It had been her mother who had laughed when she said she wanted to be a nurse, telling her that she just didn't see Dylan being able to do that. Dylan had become a doctor just to prove the woman wrong.

In her room, she slipped the unread letter into the box in her closet. Stripping off most of her clothes, she climbed into bed and opened

Holden's second letter to her. It was a drawing of a teddy bear, and in nearly unreadable writing on the bottom, he said he won the bear at a carnival for her. Ring toss, apparently.

Looking at the picture, she let sleep overtake her as she wondered what it would be like to actually go to a carnival with him. He would win all the games, she was sure of it, and she would hate all the people around.

CHAPTER 13

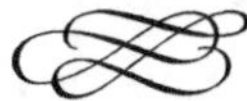

His hope of catching her before she got completely dressed for their date was a success based on her wet, loose hair and untucked shirt. Grinning at her not-perfectness as he walked into the room, he knew she was a little mad he was early. Over the weeks, he had come at precisely 5:15 p.m. on the dot. Today he was ten minutes early, which had rattled her completely, and he loved it when she was rattled.

"You're early," she sounded flustered as she started tucking in her shirt.

Grabbing the shirt, he pulled her to him for a kiss. Nothing earth-shattering; just a peck to tell her he missed her. Pushing her hands away from the hem of her shirt, he said an inch from her lip, "Leave it, Dyl, you look sexy like this."

Her grin was worth it when she replied, "You've been in the desert too long, Captain, if you think this is sexy."

"Holden." He always corrected her, and so far, she had yet to say his actual name. "I could be in the middle of Times Square on New Year's Eve and see you as sexy right now."

When she tried to protest again, he kissed her, not wanting to listen to her belittle herself. Since they'd started dating, he'd heard from her mouth every little demeaning thing anyone had said about her, only now it was coming *from* her.

Everything thing that wasn't Dylan the doctor or Dylan the surgeon never measured up to what Dylan expected of herself. She didn't eat healthy enough, run far enough, or sleep long enough. And apparently, her eyes were asymmetrical, her nose wasn't straight enough, and her legs were short.

What she never talked about was the scar that ran along her jaw or the one that cut across her lower lip, or why she had gotten her tattoos or who caused the scars on her back. Also included in that was anything that happened when she was growing up or married to his brother. All of that had been cut off from their conversations.

It was like they were sneaking around behind Chase's back. It felt like he was back in the States waiting for them to get home, not knowing that they had taken a step they shouldn't have. But every time he kissed her neck, he saw the chain that still held the ring that said Holden was not his brother.

"I have to get ready." She pushed back from him, as if she knew his brother was on his mind.

"No, you don't. We're having a picnic today."

"You do realize it is over a hundred degrees out there, right?" She glanced at the window that the sun was still beating into.

"Yes, and that's why we'll eat in here." He waved a hand at the room.

"Where? There's no room." She looked around skeptically.

Without answering, he grabbed the blanket off her bed and laid it on the floor. Though there was only five square feet of space, it was enough. After the blanket was placed, he grabbed the bag of food he had brought from the hallway and happily set it in the middle of the blanket.

Her eyes still said she wasn't buying it, that this wasn't what she considered a picnic, but the set of her mouth said she was willing to go with it...for him.

Holden quickly took off his shirt, leaving the T-shirt that matched hers, then took off his socks and shoes. They were a matching set as he took her hand and led her to the blanket.

"Supper awaits." He grinned when she sat on the blanket and arranged himself next to her, a bit too close because she tried to move away from him, but he put his arm around her and she stopped.

"What did you bring?" she asked, eyeing the bag, but not reaching for it. As always, this was his thing, and she was along for the ride.

"Look and see." He kissed her temple and wished she could get excited about things, wishing her control could be broken.

Leaning forward, she opened the bag and peered inside. With a crinkled nose she said, "I thought it would be fried chicken."

"Why?" He had no idea she even liked fried chicken; she always had a salad.

"In the movies, people always have fried chicken at their picnics," she answered with a shrug, then reached in and pulled out the cold sandwiches and salads he brought.

"How about I get chicken the next time we have a picnic where there's grass?"

"No need. I don't even really like fried chicken." She laughed. "Can you imagine how many calories are in it?"

"No, and I won't. Food is for eating, not analyzing." He gave her a ham sandwich, which she set down in front of her.

"Says the hot guy who doesn't have to fight every pound from invasion." She took out the salads from the bag.

"Hot guy, huh?" he teased her and watched her blush. It was so rare that she did, and he loved that he'd made it happen.

"Like you don't know. I bet you have a woman in every city, ex's all over the place, and every other woman swooning at your feet." She tossed the plastic silverware at him, then handed him a plate.

"Nope." He grinned and pushed all the food away, pulling her onto his lap as he leaned back against her bed. Dylan shifted around so that she was straddling him and slowly raked her fingers through his hair, smiling as she did.

Though he had a few girlfriends over the years, none had lasted more than a few weeks before he got bored with them. He was starting to think this was his longest relationship yet.

Without a word, he ran his hands up her sides and under her shirt, splaying his hands on the bare skin of her back. She was completely still as his hands trailed over her body, but he didn't move toward her breasts even though he longed to caress them again.

"What are you doing?" her voice was as breathless as he felt.

"Looking for these pounds that you keep talking about. Just as I suspected, they're all in your head." He forced his hands from her body, because if he didn't, he'd be fucking her within minutes—and she wouldn't have stopped it.

Dylan briefly touched her forehead to his and groaned, then swung off his lap and grabbed at her water. She rolled her eyes at him as she took a sip. "I have worked pretty dang hard for them not to be there—that's why I run."

"Who told you that you were fat, Dylan?" he asked, because every one of her insecurities came from someone else's mouth.

"Nobody, so let's drop it," she requested, as she always did when he was getting too close to learning anything about her.

"Was it Chase?" Just because his brother was dead didn't mean he could have been a dick when alive.

"Of course not. He..." She stopped talking and reached for her sandwich.

"Please tell me." Holden took the sandwich and unwrapped it for her, then handed it back.

"He... He was the first person to ever love me for me, okay? He didn't care that I wasn't perfect, that I was weird, or that I was me. He never said that it was baby fat, or that I was big-boned, or that I should watch what I eat... He loved me anyway. I keep the weight off because my job states I must, but it isn't always easy." She grabbed the sandwich away from him but didn't take a bite of it.

"Your parents then," he surmised, nodding to himself.

"I was never perfect enough for them. I tried, but I never achieved the level of perfection they were looking for. Good grades were nice, but I was never a cheerleader or on the softball team. I was never the beautiful athletic kid that looked good in all the pictures. I was short and fat and not perfect."

"Are you still estranged from them?" He didn't have to ask; there were a hundred unopened envelopes in her closet that shouted yes.

"I've built a life without them," she admitted, which surprised him. He didn't think she would.

"Why are you still trying to be perfect for them?"

She scoffed. "I am not."

"Dylan, I have seen your underwear drawer. Everything in your life is perfect. The moment he becomes imperfect, you walk away."

She closed her eyes and arched her brows as she said, "I don't walk away from anything."

"You haven't had a real relationship in fifteen years because you can't control another person. You're scared that they'll become messy… That I'll become messy."

"I happen to have loved my husband very much," she argued back.

He looked up from the blanket between them and stared at her intently. "So much that you can't love again?"

"You don't know what you are talking about."

"I might not. I've never loved like that."

He then redirected the conversation, because if he didn't, she would kick him out. She had finally started opening up to him, and he didn't want to push her too far. "How was Elissa today?"

"She's going home in three weeks and is practically walking on air. All she talks about is Todd this and Todd that and sex, sex, sex. She's *so* ready to go home." The anger in her eyes had vanished while talking about her friend.

"What happens when she's gone? When do you leave?" He didn't really want to know, but he needed to. Maybe it was soon. Would they have enough time?

Dylan sighed. "I'll get a new nurse; she isn't my first. I've really enjoyed my time with her, though. I'll be here for probably another year, maybe more if I can get past the med boards."

"It's not healthy to stay in a war zone for years on end."

"I'm fine; I thrive here. I hate knowing what's coming next."

"What if you don't pass your next medical board?"

"Then I'll go back to the States, probably to some base somewhere. I'll still be a surgeon, but it won't be the same. How about you? Are you a lifer?"

"Oh yeah. I have no idea what I would do if I wasn't in the Army. My dad works construction, but I don't know if I can work with him."

"I thought he was dead?"

"Nope, just an ass sometimes. He's still miffed I joined the Army like Chase, since he got himself killed over it."

"He and Marquez used to have the biggest shouting contests. Your dad usually lost those, but then Marquez would be pissed for days."

"I know how he feels. I have had my own shouting matches with the man. Sometimes I wish Chase hadn't wrecked the Army by dying in it. I've always wondered if Mom and Dad would've been happier about it if he hadn't died over here."

"It's hard losing someone close to you."

"Yeah, it is," he said, tossing his trash in the bag—she had cleaned hers up as she ate. Holden offered her a quick smile as he stood up, then held out his hand to her. "I have a surprise for you."

Once on her feet, she looked at him quizzically. "What kind of surprise?"

"Now that we've had an amazing picnic, I'm taking you to a movie."

"Where at?" she asked, eyes brightening a little.

"Right here," he replied and pulled out his phone and waved it at her. "I had one of my guys download a new release today."

"On the floor again?" Her eyes were on the blanket still lying next to her bed.

"No silly, in bed. But only because you don't have a couch." He shut off her light since the sun had only started to set it was still very light in the room.

Grabbing the blanket, he sat against the headboard and patted the spot beside him. He realized his error as soon as she climbed in next to him. It was a twin bed, and there wasn't enough room for them to sit side-by-side. His plan was to snuggle close to her, but this was too close, and he felt like he was going to fall off the bed.

As the movie started up, he re-situated them and so that her body was between his knees. Pulling the blanket around them both, she rested her head against his chest, letting the smell of roses surround him.

After about four minutes into the movie, he realized the men in his group were shitheads, and not one of them understood what his plan was with Dylan because that was the moment the main female character in the movie took off her bra, by accident. *Are you kidding me, guys?!* The "movie" they had put on his phone was a porno!

So much for a movie night where he didn't constantly think about having sex with her. No. Instead, he had to watch raunchy sex with her in his arms. He could stop the movie, but he had nothing else planned and would probably just have to leave. With her in his arms, though, he didn't want to.

As he was thinking over his options, he could feel Dylan laughing silently against his chest. Amazingly, she was taking it in stride, not saying anything about the "movie" they were watching.

Then the guy's pants came off, and she laughed and said, "Well, that's a disappointment."

"Expecting more, Dyl?" he whispered into her hair.

"Uh, yeah, and so should Babs. So much more."

"The director was maybe more concerned with how Babs looked than Ronnie."

"I can see that, since her name is practically boobs, and Ronnie? Why not Rod or Willy or Johnson? Obviously, Hollywood isn't focusing on the right thing." So far, she hadn't taken her eyes off of the tiny screen, only wiggling closer to him as the movie went on.

"Never heard it called a 'Ronnie' before?"

"Nope, and I've worked around fowl-mouthed soldiers for over a decade. I know all the euphemisms."

"All?" he asked with a laugh. He could tell she was having fun.

"When I was in Iraq on my first tour, I worked with three doctors that had been together for a long time. They always called each other 'dick' in every way possible. I think they thought it would embarrass me, but I held it together."

"I'll have to test your knowledge one day." He hugged her tighter to him.

Dylan was still holding up the phone, so he took the opportunity to snake his hands under her shirt. He caressed her stomach and sides ever so slowly, and he could feel her relaxing into his hands. When she let out a soft moan of approval, he cupped her breasts, running his thumbs over the lace of her bra. She sighed, and her head fell back into his chest.

There was no way she didn't feel his rock-hard shaft digging into her back. It had been there before the movie had started, and he didn't need the movie to keep it there. As his hand slid under her bra, she adjusted herself against his chest, intentionally rubbing her back into his cock.

"Did he just…" she trailed off, her eyes on the screen.

He kissed her ear, then softly bit it before whispering, "He did."

It was almost full-on dark now, with the only light in the room being his phone, flickering sex scenes right at them. Her knees inched apart, and she ground her back even more into his cock while thrusting her breasts into his hand.

On the screen, the couple was fully into it, making wild sounds Holden had actually never heard during sex. But in their bed, they were both silent as church mice as he continued to worship her breasts.

"Here, hold the phone," she whispered, shaking it a little as if to get his attention.

"Why?" He licked her ear this time, and her body trembled.

"I need to…" She didn't say, just shook the phone again. His thumbs stopped circling her nipples and slid out of her bra and down her stomach, making her suck it in enough for him to get a hand under the waistband of her pants.

"In a minute." His hand slipped over her wet panties, which caused her to gasp.

She rocked her hips over his erection. "Please."

With a grin, he pulled his hand out and brought it down the front of her pants and cupped her core. Her breath caught, and she moaned a low *"yes"* as he rubbed her gently through the layers of fabric. With his other hand, he undid her pants, earning him another breathy moan.

Holden brought his hand up and then back into her pants as her knees separated a bit more. Dylan's hands were shaking again, but not with impatience anymore. She bucked against him when he found his target, and a low growl of approval rumbled through his chest at how wet and ready she was.

While running a hand over her clit, he watched her hands holding the screen aloft. His finger slowly went back and forth as the screen shook, but she held on. Picking up his speed, he saw her knees starting to shake also. Good thing he wasn't interested in the movie— Dylan had dropped it and was now digging her fingers into his thighs.

Her entire body tensed the moment before she dropped the phone and rolled her head back and forth, moaning. His free hand snaked back up and squeezed her breast, flicking a thumb across her nipple as her orgasm hit, forcing his name from her lips.

He wrapped his arms around her and held her tight as she tried to catch her breath.

"I dropped the phone," she said for no reason. They both knew why.

"I think it was over anyway." He had no idea and didn't care at all.

As if realizing it was still in bed with them, she sat up and found his phone. After turning off the movie, she placed it on the nightstand and rolled over, climbing up his body until she was straddling him. Gently, she took his face in her hands.

Grinning, she asked, "Can we please fuck now? Romance is all good and great, but a lady has needs."

He grabbed her face as well. "A man hates to be used for his body. Will you let me make love to you?"

"*Men.* Always so needy." She winked at him and laughed.

"Yes or no, Dylan? Will you let me?" All humor was gone from his voice. This time was going to be different. This time wasn't about getting off.

She dropped her hands to his shoulders and looked at him for a second. "Yes."

"What's my name?" His own hands had dropped to his side, not even touching her anymore.

"Captain Marquez." Her lopsided grin said she knew exactly what he was asking of her.

"First name? The name I want you to call me," he demanded, eyes intent on hers.

"Holden. Your name is Holden."

"I love it when you say my name, Dyl." His mouth landed on hers, but neither touched the other with anything but their lips.

With her position on above him, she slid off her shirt and unclasped her bra, letting his eyes feast on her breasts. His hands cupped them, and she moaned.

Her hands were busy with his shirt and pants, pushing them off as best she could while he was still under her.

"I think we just have to get undressed. This bed is too small," he said as he unbuttoned her pants.

Leveraging herself on his chest, she got to her feet. Within seconds, she was naked. It took him longer since he was wearing more clothes than her, but he got to enjoy the view as she waited for him on the bed. She felt the same way as she watched him slowly undress as well.

The moment his underwear hit the floor, she scooted back to make room for him, though there would never be enough room for him in her tiny bed. His lips claimed hers, and her hands reached around him and pulled him closer, both needing to feel the other completely.

As his hands roamed over her body, she managed to find a condom and rolled it onto him, even as her hands caressed him.

It had been weeks of buildup, and his body wasn't waiting, despite all his inner chants of taking it slow. Once she was there, he couldn't stop.

After slipping into her, she wrapped her legs around him and held him tight to her for a moment. Then she kissed him as her hips began to rock, starting a rhythm.

"Dylan, I want to take our time." His hips stilled as he spoke.

"Fuck, Holden, next time. This time I just need you, now." Her hips bucked again.

At the sound of his name, he let go and pounded into her, sending wave after wave of orgasm through her. By the time he crested, he had no idea how many she'd had, just that she wasn't stopping. Her walls gripped his cock tighter and tighter with each thrust until he couldn't stop himself from coming.

Drained, he pulled her to his chest and tried to steady his breathing. He was surprised when she went willingly, but she murmured something he couldn't hear and snuggled into him farther.

It was completely different from the first time they had been together. This time wasn't just sex, it was something more. But Holden couldn't help but wondering if this was something that Dylan truly wanted.

CHAPTER 14

GOING BACK to work after spending nearly an entire day in bed with Holden wasn't easy. All she could think about was getting back to him and being with him again. Her shift was nearly half over, and she was counting the hours, but there was still a long way to go.

"Earth to Dylan," Elissa said beside her, holding files for patients that needed to be signed. "Well, someone's in a sex fog today."

"And what do you know of sex fogs?" She took the files from her.

"I know I have two and a half weeks before my next one. I'm glad to see that romance has spread to the bedroom for you. You seem happy now."

"I'm always happy," she countered.

Elissa gave her a skeptical look. "Rarely, ever so rarely."

Dylan was thinking about a good comeback when their phones chimed in unison—time to get to work.

Getting up, they both headed for the OR. Elissa was quicker though, and was already in the room when she stepped inside.

"IED blast, most of the damage is to his back, but his spine seems okay," Elissa said, but the usual cheeriness that she brought with her was gone. Sure, it wasn't a place for fun, but blood and gore couldn't dominate everything in the OR.

While pulling on a glove, Dylan looked at the soldier on her table. The man was lying on his stomach, and his back was a bloody mess. She wondered if he was conscious when they sedated him; probably not. Looking over the damage, her mind went into autopilot and created a plan. Elissa handed her a scalpel that she didn't need to ask for, and she touched her soldier's skin tentatively.

The tingle that shot through her arm at the mere touch had her pulling back for an instant and looking at her friend, whose only answer was a nod. The soldier on her table was the same one she had woken up to yesterday morning: Holden.

Her eyes went wide with shock, but then she shook her head to refocus. Pushing Holden from her mind, she mindlessly worked on him for hours, sewing him back together as best she could and trying to leave as little scaring as possible.

As she tied the last suture closed, she knew she was saying goodbye to him; he wouldn't be conscious again in Afghanistan. All of his recovery would be elsewhere this time. She also knew he was never coming back—the injury was career-ending.

As most of the surgical staff left the room to work on someone else, she went around and looked at his face. He looked like he was sleeping. She knew that look. Kissing his dirty, sandy cheek, she whispered her goodbyes and went to wash his blood from her body.

Hours later, she was still in her office with the lights off, trying to stop seeing his bloody body in her mind. It was pointless—she would see it until the day she died. He had somehow wormed his way into her heart, and now he was gone.

With a soft knock, Elissa came into the room and whispered, "Ambulance just took him to the airport. Germany first."

"I know." She had signed the transfer papers.

"He's probably done." Elissa somehow knew everything.

"I know," she said again. What else was there?

"You still have his address, Dylan. You can write." She nodded at the papers on her desk. His was there somewhere, but Dylan couldn't look at it. Not yet, maybe one day.

"It's over, Elissa. It was always over when one of us left."

"It doesn't have to be."

"Yes, it does," she stated firmly and pushed past her friend. She needed out of this room and away from this conversation.

Somehow, she managed to hold back the tears until she made it back to her room the next morning. She might have even saved them until after she slept, except he had left her flowers on the bed, the one she had left him sleeping in. They were in a vase and written in black pen. He'd signed it: *Thinking of you, Holden.* Hugging the papers to her chest, she sobbed for the man who was as dead to her as his brother was, who had touched her heart and made her believe in life again.

❧

SITTING HURT, standing hurt, breathing hurt, thinking hurt. Getting shot in the leg last month had been a breeze compared to this. It had been weeks, and he still felt like it just happened. His mind was still there, surviving.

One minute he was with his guys in the desert and the next, he was in Germany and in pain. There was no memory of what happened in between those moments. That much he was grateful for. He had lost two good men that day and two others had been seriously injured, like him.

At least the bomb hadn't been an IED—it had been a vest of explosives strapped to a young local they thought that they could trust. They had been wrong. Maybe if he hadn't been thinking about Dylan, he would have noticed the kid was acting weird earlier. Maybe if he hadn't been consumed by her, he would've had his head in the game.

Instead, he had been lost in thought when he should have been protecting his men, and he had paid the price. The pain in his back wasn't his worst pain right now.

"How are you feeling today, Captain?" the doctor asked. Holden had decided he didn't care who the doctor was; they weren't going to fix anything.

"Great, never better."

"Good to hear." The man didn't joke around much. "I'm guessing that you should be able to head home in about a month."

The man made it sound like it was a good thing to be sent home. A good thing to have to start a life where he couldn't do what he loved. A good thing to have to move in with his mother, who was going to complain about the Army hurting him, and that he deserved it.

"Thought you'd be more excited." The doctor wrote something in his file, probably something about him being depressed.

"I want to be where I belong—with my team, but we both know I'll never go back again. The Army's done with me," he hissed. He couldn't even lean back in his bed, much less carry a gun over his back.

"You're not going back, but that doesn't mean you have to leave the Army. There are other jobs."

"I am not sitting at a desk all day." He knew his limits.

"How about you talk to your CO? Maybe they have some ideas of places you could go?"

"The government wants soldiers, Doc, not people doing nothing." He didn't add "people like you," but should have. The man had done little since Holden had gotten there. Other doctors had done the bulk of the work.

"It takes people doing nothing, as you say, to support those that are fighting. You still have a place if you want a place. You just have to want it."

As the doctor walked away, probably to torment another used-up soldier, he looked out the window. All he saw was blue sky; his angle didn't allow him a view of the ground.

"Hey, Captain, how's it going?" A female voice came from the door. The blond hair was tied back, and she was holding her hat under her arm.

Squinting at her in the green fatigues, he couldn't place her at all, though the voice was familiar. Without being asked, she walked into the room and looked at his back since he had no shirt on. There was no need with all the bandages on it.

"Did that bomb blow away your memory?" she asked, poking at his back a little bit.

"Sorry, can't place you," he admitted, hoping like hell she wasn't someone he'd dated.

"Really? I help you get into Dylan's pants, and you promptly forget me? Next time, you're out of luck."

"Elissa?" He looked at her again and saw it this time. He had never seen her in anything but scrubs, and just like with Dylan, had forgotten she was actually in the Army.

"Good job, sir. Only a little rattled." She flicked his ear before sitting down in the chair by the bed.

"What are you going here?" he asked. She was in the wrong country if she was heading home.

"Heading home, but we had to come through here first. Never question the military. When I found out you were still here, I decided to stop by and visit. You know, catch up." She was as cheerful here as she had been there.

"Welcome to my hell."

"You'll heal."

He gave her a flat look. "Not enough."

"Better than dead. Dead is *always* worse."

"Some days, I wish."

"I guess this is why Dylan hated patient visits. They are such a downer."

"I suppose you want me to ask about her?"

"Up to you. I'm not going to tell if you don't ask," she admitted.

"Not going to ask."

She shrugged. "We caught your call. She sewed you back together. Knew it was you without asking. There's something still there between you two."

"It's over."

Elissa's eyes turned downward, shoulders slumping a little. "As she said."

"Where's home?"

"Suburbs of Chicago. Husband and a kid, I get to go back to that. Last deployment, too. No more re-upping."

"Sounds great."

"It is. Unlike you, I haven't had sex in over a year and cannot *wait* to get home." She laughed at her answer.

Holden felt a smile pulling at the corner of his mouth. "I can see why Dylan loved working with you."

"She worked with me because I'm the best. She doesn't take second-best."

"Me neither, which is why we would never work. I can't compete with a ghost."

"You mean her late husband? He's just an excuse to not get close to anyone."

"Well, it works."

"A man just has to work hard for her. You know she's worth it."

"How is she going to get by without you?"

Her smile fell at his words. "She doesn't have to. She was sent back to the States on medical leave until further notice…burnout. She was gone within a week of you."

"Shit," he hissed under his breath. At this point, he had no idea what she was doing if she wasn't working.

"Your injury might not have only ended your career, Captain, it might've been the straw that broke the camel's back for Dylan."

"Are you blaming that on me?"

"No! She drove herself to the edge; you just were the wind that pushed her over. She was going to fall sometime, anyway. I'm kind of glad it happened before I left, so I didn't have to worry about her."

"She really liked working with you also."

"We were a good team. I'm really going to miss her. The desert, though? No." She chuckled.

"I'm going to miss it all."

"Maybe you can find something better than sand. Dylan's back somewhere in the States and will be for a while. You can *romance* her again."

"I doubt she would want someone like me."

"I don't think she will settle for anyone but you, Captain. She might still wear his ring, but he doesn't have her heart anymore."

"It's his name tattooed on her arm."

"As is yours." Elissa patted his shoulder lightly as she left the room, her blond hair swaying as she did.

CHAPTER 15

"WE ARE STARTING our descent and will be landing in Minneapolis in thirty minutes. The local time is 8:15 p.m., and the temperature is thirty-five degrees," the pilot announced, as if half an hour was long enough for her to come to grips with returning to where Dylan had come from.

When she'd gotten on a bus at eighteen, she had said goodbye to this place. She had no plans of ever returning. And now, she was in a steel tube, barreling right at it.

Last week, she had returned to a country she hadn't seen in two years. It hadn't changed. But her return had meant a full physical, from her body to her mind. Neither made the medical board happy.

Her mind was shot, and the shaking in her hand wasn't controllable anymore. Even now in the middle of a flight, it was trembling on her lap. Grabbing it with her other hand to make it stop, she looked out the tiny window into the darkness.

A three-month leave was her sentence; three months of doing nothing was her price to pay. Once those three months were up, she would meet before the board again to plead for her job back.

Not that her body was doing any better than her mind. She was twenty pounds too light and had no appetite. What little she ate, she threw up just as fast. Running hadn't been an option since Holden's accident; her mind wasn't clearing anymore. All she saw was his mangled body, and at night in her dreams, she couldn't fix the damage.

The lights of the city below them came into view, and she wondered if anyone was going to meet her when she got off the plane. Had her mom been told she was coming home? Would they ignore all the notes in her file to not tell her unless she was dead? Would they both be there: Janet and her perfect Jenna?

Dylan ran her hands over her face, forcing the images of the imaginary reunion from her mind. She was here to rest. Her CO had sent her home, but she was in no way *going* home. Tonight, she would find a hotel and from there, she would decide what she wanted to do.

"My wife wants you to know that we're proud of you." The voice came from the burly guy beside her who had been silent the entire flight from Texas. The only words they had spoken the entire three hours they had been together had been when she asked for the window seat.

Looking around him, she saw a skinnier guy on the other side reading. No wife in site.

"Um, she's at home. I'm on a business trip, so she couldn't come along," he explained nervously at her questioning look.

"Thank you, I think?" she said in confusion. She had never had a stranger say they were proud of her. Thanked her, sure, but never this.

"Our son Wyatt joined up when he was eighteen. It pissed us off to no end, but that was how he was. What we wanted for him had never mattered—he had a mind of his own. The Army, it grew him up like nothing we could've done. They made him into a man. He was killed before we could tell him; before he came home again." Seeing the tears swimming in the big man's eyes, Dylan couldn't help but wonder if the guy had been on her table? Had she not saved him?

"Sorry about your son," she said words she had never had to in all of her years of being a doctor. She had never faced a grieving parent and was grateful for that now.

"Me and the Mrs. decided that whenever we see a soldier from then on to tell them we are proud of them. We didn't get the chance with Wyatt, and everyone deserves to be told."

"You don't even know if I have done anything to be proud of." Maybe his son hadn't died at her hands, but others had. She didn't even know the numbers anymore.

"Have you done something for me to be proud of, Major?" he questioned her.

"I hope so, sir. I sure hope so."

She let the dead fall away and wondered how many were alive today because of her. How many got to hear again that their parents were proud of them? Loved them?

"You going home?"

"I guess. This is where I'm from."

"Do your parents know you are coming?"

"No," she admitted, not that she would tell this man that it was because her mother couldn't be proud of her. She wasn't perfect enough for that. And now she was nothing.

Her dad was long dead. He'd died young, but Dylan didn't know and didn't care how. His family was not a part of her life.

"They'll be so excited to see you." The guy nearly laughed at the excitement. Dylan didn't even crack a smile.

"I'm sure they will be." She faked a smile for him—they were not going to see her.

"Do you need a lift?"

"No, thank you. I have a ride. You go home to your wife; she misses you."

"You married?"

"I was once, a long time ago." She tried to come up with images of Marquez, but his brother's face was all she could think of now. That and his mangled body.

"Sorry about your loss." He took her hand and squeezed it.

"Can I just sit here a moment?" she asked as the plane was emptying, and he was staying with her.

"Yeah, sure." He got up and grabbed his bag from over their seats, saying, "I hope your parents give you a big hug, because if I were your dad, I wouldn't let you go."

"For that, I wish you were my dad. Go home and hug your older boys. They need it too." She turned away from him, not wanting to see his tears for the kids he loved.

Staring out at the airport lights, she knew he watched her for a while before leaving, but she was done talking. Done with people for a long time.

Now was the time to think about her future; a future that might not include sand and destroyed young bodies. What was she supposed to do without work and exhaustion?

"Major, the plane has landed," a flight attendant stated. He was tall and good-looking and had obviously drawn the short straw. He looked at the forward cabin nervously.

"Yes, I know. Thank you," she said and climbed over the two seats to get out of her hole.

Dylan grabbed her bag, Army-issue of course, and tossed it over her shoulder. It contained almost everything that she owned. The rest was in a storage unit in California, where she had finished her residency. If Marquez's things weren't in it, she would have just abandoned it.

Walking off the plane, she tried not to notice the stares she was getting from the rest of the crew, the ones who got the long straws. Yes, she knew she looked like crap, but did they have to stare at her?

Once in the airport, she saw the sign for transportation and followed the arrow. Passing a food vendor, she thought about stopping but didn't feel like eating. She hadn't felt like eating in such a long time.

As she walked, she kept an eye out for any signs that her mother was there, that word had gotten out that she was home, but nobody seemed to notice her or pay much attention to her.

By the time she had made it to the car rental desk, she was happy she hadn't run into anyone from her past. With keys to a little compact car in her hand, she headed for the restroom before heading out to her three months of who knows what.

Sitting down in a stall, she stared straight into her own blue eyes. The stall door had a sign with her mother's picture on it. After twenty years, Dylan knew it was her mother. The person smiling beside her had to be Jenna, all grown up and looking like her mother. The caption beside them said: Welcome home.

Scanning the advertisement, she realized her mother and sister were now real estate agents. Her stomach twisted at seeing their faces. They weren't welcoming her back—just everyone else.

Slamming out of the stall, she knew she needed out of this town as soon as possible. She had three months before she had to be back and wouldn't spend them here at all.

Forty miles away from the airport, she still hadn't turned off the highway. With no destination in mind, she just drove, past unfamiliar, nearly foreign sites after so long away from the States.

Another town approached, and she finally pulled over to eat. Her timer had gone off just as she had left the airport, reminding her to eat. Pulling off the highway, she picked the first drive-thru she found and ordered the first thing on the menu. It didn't matter what it was; she didn't taste any of it anyway.

But for now, she had to eat. Not for her, but for Holden. For the next seven months, everything she did to her body would be for Holden and his child that she was carrying. A child she had no right to raise. A little soul that didn't need a mother like her in its life. Holden would raise it and be the perfect parent with whatever wife he found.

After the baby was gone, she could go back and work until she couldn't anymore. Then her life would be over.

CHAPTER 16

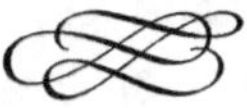

"Is being in the Army hard?" the kid asked. He was scrawny and hadn't worked a day in all of his eighteen years, Holden was sure of that.

"Yes, it's a physical job," he said, wanting to tell the kid to just leave, because he wasn't joining the Army. This was all a waste of time.

"I can do physical work, but hard work, I don't know." As if there was actually a difference.

Holden barely held back an eyeroll, telling himself that at least he was still in the Army. It had been months—long, hard, painful months since some kid tried to blow him to pieces.

Behind him, where the kid couldn't see, Jake David did roll his eyes. Jake had turned into a great friend in the last two months. They even were starting to think alike.

"To tell you the truth, Jaden, if you join the Army, you will be in the best shape of your life within three months. You'll be ripped and toned, and the chicks won't be able to leave you alone. But if you would rather play video games, do that."

"But isn't the Army like a video game?" he asked, his eyes a little brighter now.

"No, the Army is not like a game. You get up every day and do what you are told, no matter what. And you get shot at sometimes." A little scare tactic.

"But I get a gun, too, so I can shoot them back?"

"No, that's not the way it works. How about you take a few more days and think about it? Talk to your parents and friends and make sure it's what you want," Holden said, hoping to God he never saw the kid again.

"Okay." The kid hopped up and left the office full of excitement.

He forgot to tell the kid that you lose friends and family. And that when you get hurt, you might not heal. Even today, the skin on his back pulled when he twisted. It wasn't exactly pain, but it wasn't nothing either.

"Guns and video games, that's all they think the Army is." Jake got up and looked out the plate-glass window at the street and watched the snow fall.

Holden had been lucky enough to get assigned to the recruiting station he had signed up at. It was close to home, and he had found a little house not far. Living with his parents at thirty-one had been too difficult, no matter how injured he was.

"I know. No one says they just want to see the desert and be shot at every day." Holden ran his fingers through his hair that was no longer just stubble, but an actual style. One he had just messed up.

"One day."

Jake hadn't said his wife was home today, but Holden always knew when Mara was home for the day, because Jake got antsy. Not that he didn't trust his wife or something; he just liked to be there when she was.

They had met in high school and had been together ever since. Both had joined the Army and been deployed on and off over their twelve years of marriage. Now they were both here, her retired and him working with Holden. They had two kids and a dog and couldn't stand being apart, even for work.

"Mara off today?" he asked, because Jake loved to talk about her.

"No, she's working all day. We had a fight this morning about laundry." Jake was still looking at the snow. Mara was a nurse at the VA hospital. It wasn't a war zone, but it wasn't the safest place either.

"She'll be okay," Holden assured him, seeing the worry in his friend's face.

"I hate fighting with her," Jake admitted, not saying that it might be the last thing they said to each other. War makes every day special.

"Send her flowers or leave early and do all the damned laundry in the house." Holden grinned. He may not have a woman, but he still knew how to treat one.

Romance, even the word, made his chest ache. He had never checked to see where Dylan was. He could, an address was easily obtainable, but he didn't.

Though he was sure she was stateside, he didn't look. She was still in love with his brother, and Holden was still in love with her. Sometimes he wished he could go back and grab the ring from her hand and throw it away, demanding that she love him, but it wasn't his name that was tattooed on her arm, that was his brother's too.

"It was about her not cleaning up the laundry. I'm already in charge of it, but my beautiful, amazing wife is a pig." He sat down at his desk and looked at the picture of the bubbly redhead there.

"Then tell her to leave work early and do all the laundry." He laughed, though even to him, it sounded forced.

"Sorry to talk about Mara so much, I know you're hurting." Jake's face sobered.

"My back is doing okay today." He pretended to be confused. One night of drinking had him spilling his guts about Dylan. Not everything, but enough.

"I could tell you where she is," his friend offered, not for the first time.

"No need. We're over. It was a convenience thing…when we were close," he said, trying to make it sound like less than it was. Because to him, it had been the best relationship he had ever been in, even if it had been difficult and not truly real. He wanted her back.

"I think it went beyond that."

"Let it drop," Holden mumbled, trying to stop seeing her laughing eyes as they picnicked in her little room.

"Take Mara on a picnic," he said a moment later. It had worked for him, after all.

"It's snowing." Jake didn't seem to hate the idea; he just didn't get it.

"Do it in the house. Put down a blanket and have a picnic the moment she gets home." He smiled at his friend, but his heart broke a little more at the memory.

"Holden, you're brilliant. She gets off after the kids are in bed." Jake was already planning when a girl walked into the office. Her black hair and dark eyes spoke of her Hispanic roots. Her accent said it too.

"This the Army place?" she asked both of them, not concerned that they were two men and she was a young girl. She had balls.

"It is. Are you looking for the Army?" In four words, she had impressed him more than Jaden had in an entire conversation.

"I am." She turned to him, leaving Jake out of the conversation.

He gestured for her to sit down. "What can the Army do for you?"

"College and a career."

"What do you want to be?"

"A lawyer," she said with confidence, a confidence he often saw in Dylan. Had she said "doctor" when she walked into an office like this? Had she even known she wanted to be a doctor?

"And you want to go through the Army to get that? Basic? Combat? A lot of hassle for a degree you can get without it," he replied, his eye on Jake, who was on the phone. Based on the smile, he was talking with his wife.

She shook her head. "No, no, I can't. I need the help. I am willing to do the work."

"Can I get you to fill out some forms for me? Now, this doesn't sign you up, but it'll be a start." He handed over the forms for a background check and other basic information that was needed.

"Marquez, I have a phone call for you." Jake was holding the phone in the air.

"I am with this young lady," Holden couldn't help the irritation in his voice. He shouldn't have had to point that out since they were still in the same office.

"Phone, Marquez, now." He got up and was still holding the phone, eyes insistent.

Getting up, Holden went and grabbed the phone and watched Jake take over with the girl, something he had never done before. With his heart in his throat, he thought about his brother Lane, who was on a ship somewhere in the Pacific. His dad and other brother, Roark, were working somewhere in the city on a building project. Someone was injured.

"Holden Marquez," he barked into the phone. He wasn't ready to hear that anyone was injured or dead.

"Holden, it's Mara. Stop yelling at me," she said in a whisper.

"What do you want?" She had never called him before. In fact, they had spoken very little to each other, no matter how much he knew about her.

"I am at work."

"Yes, at the VA." He already knew that—Jake had already mentioned it about a dozen times that day.

"Okay, so Jake told me about your girlfriend," she admitted, still whispering.

"He shouldn't have."

"Too late. Anyway, I'm in the ER today, and a few minutes ago, one of the doctors was found in the parking lot. Slipped on the ice and fell. We think she was unconscious for a while. Anyway, she came through here."

"And you are telling me because…?"

"Because her name is Dylan Marquez—isn't that the woman's name? And she's a doctor." Mara's voice got louder, then really quiet.

Now it was Holden's turn to whisper. "Yes, but I don't think she's here."

"I took a snap of her ID and sent it to Jake," she said quickly and paused, as if giving him time to get the phone from his friend. Who handed it to him immediately. *Seriously?* He shot a bewildered look at Jake.

The photo was blurry, but not so blurry that he couldn't tell it was Dylan. She was wearing a white coat over her Army greens in the photo. His heartbeat started quickening; she had fallen and had lain in the cold for who knows how long.

Questions bombarded him. Why she was here? How long had she

been here? Why hadn't she looked for him? Had she looked for him, but didn't want to see him?

"It's her, isn't it? Not many girls named Dylan out there." Mara sounded smug.

"It's her. Is she conscious yet?" He needed to know.

"I don't know, she was through here pretty quickly, but I talked to a friend who works in OB and she said…" Mara took a breath finally.

"OB?" He was trying to stay with the conversation, but his mind was yelling at him to drive over and see her.

"She said they're doing a C-section. Immediately. You have to come," she demanded at full vocal range.

Holden's mind went completely blank. What did she say?

"I…maybe looked at her file online, and she lists you as the daddy." She was back to whispering. "Shit, car accident, have to go."

The woman hung up on him, but he was already out the door before the phone hit the top of Jake's desk. Dylan was here and having a baby? Nothing made sense, but he was going to VA to find out.

The drive was a blur, and he had no idea how he got to the hospital. Running through the doors, the receptionist looked at his uniform and let him know where Dylan's room was. On the third floor, he flagged down a nurse who had him suited up in the gauzy material Dylan always wore.

"Just in time," a woman stated from the other side of a curtain, but his eyes were glued to the woman on the table.

It had been months, but she looked the same. She looked like she was dead, all peaceful and relaxed. He wondered if she was still as tense as she used to be. Holden gently touched her hand to make sure she was still warm. Her skin was still as soft as before. All he could do was touch her and tell her everything was going to be okay.

Running his hand up her shoulder, he dislodged the paper gown that was covering her. After straightening it, he realized she didn't have her dog tags on her, which she wouldn't; she was in the States, so she didn't need them anymore. But she also was missing the necklace that held Chase's ring. Had the hospital taken it off? Had she?

A nurse hurried over to him and began filling him in. "She did regain consciousness, but we sedated her anyway. Once the baby is out, and she's in recovery, she should come out of it just fine."

"Baby?" he asked in confusion. He was so focused on Dylan that he had forgotten about the life they had created.

"Dr. Nicholas is working on it now. Since we didn't know what happened out there, we decided it was safer to just get the baby out. She was already at 38 weeks, so not a big deal." The nurse checked a few things on Dylan, like Dylan always did with her patients.

"How long are they supposed to be?" He had never cared before, but now needed to know everything. *He was going to be a dad?*

"Forty," she answered as a baby started to cry, loud angry wails. His baby.

"You have a son. Congratulations," the doctor announced, and within seconds, the nurse was back with a red, screaming baby boy. The kid was obviously not happy to be there, but Holden couldn't believe how close he had come to missing this moment.

CHAPTER 17

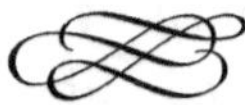

"...AND Daddy is with the baby. You have one excited man there, Doc," the nurse stated as she checked all the readouts from the machines. Dylan could have told her everything was good. Everything but her baby's daddy being there.

Though she had been conscious for a half an hour at that point, she still hadn't pieced together how Holden had found her, much less found her while she was delivering their son. Or, at least she thought the nurse meant Holden. She had yet to see him.

"Yeah." Was all she could say. He should be pissed, not excited.

Closing her eyes, she wondered how he had found her. After landing in Minneapolis months before, she had immediately taken her car and drove. Within a week, she had stopped and bought a new car and put ten thousand miles on it. By the time she drove back into town, she was at peace in some ways.

When she had joined the Army, she wanted to see the world. After twenty years of service, she had finally seen the country she had defended. From the Midwest to the South, across the deserts of the southwest and Washington state. She had hit state parks and national ones, seeing things she had only read about.

Then she had cleaned out the storage unit she had been paying on for fifteen years. Most of it was now trash, but some of it had been brought to the little apartment she was renting.

Her last stop before coming back was at Arlington National Cemetery to see Marquez. Sadly, she had talked to him for hours, telling him everything. She had started to show by then, but she needed his forgiveness.

Walking away from his grave, she knew he wasn't there, despite all her talking. He had known from the beginning, and maybe he had even approved from the beginning. Leaving his ring on the headstone, she knew she couldn't keep wearing it with another man's child growing in her. And after fifteen years, she needed to stop pretending Chase was the reason she was broken. She was already broken when they met.

Her meeting with the review board had gone splendidly, they had approved for her to be back in the OR. Since she wasn't able to go back to Afghanistan, she had requested a position in Minneapolis because that was where Holden was. It would make it easier to hand off the baby if they lived in the same city.

Once Holden had the baby, she could look for a different job elsewhere. Somewhere no one knew her or knew that she hadn't been brave enough to raise her own child.

If she could move, she would leave the hospital now. Holden was with the baby and happy. They would be happy together...without her.

"Look who's awake, Junior," the man himself said from the door, carrying a bundle of blankets in his arms.

"Mr. Marquez, you cannot just take the baby." A different nurse was right behind him. This one was older and madder than the one attending Dylan.

"He asked to see his mommy. How could I say no?" Holden was smiling from ear to ear as he shook off the woman.

"There are rules," she stated.

"And they are?" Holden turned on her.

"The baby must be in its bed when moving through the hallway." Her hands went to her hips.

"We *are* in a room," Holden argued, as if he hadn't just made the journey to get there on foot.

"Don't do it again," she hissed, then left the room.

Holden turned back to Dylan, a huge smile on his face. His hair was longer, and he looked a little less bulky, but *God* he looked amazing.

"Mommy's up!" he whispered excitedly to the baby as he walked to her bed.

Dylan tried to control the flutter in her heart when she heard those words. She didn't need attachment at this point with either of them. They'd be better off without her.

"Hey, Mommy, you should see this amazing little guy you've been cooking for so long." He sat down on the edge of the bed and tilted the bundle toward her.

All she could see was a little face and big blue eyes—he was looking back at her. From where she was, she couldn't see either herself or Holden in his features. Just a baby with dark hair and blue eyes that seemed to judge her. Both came from his father.

"I don't know what to say," she admitted. Where to start?

"Just say hi," he whispered. His warm hand touched her chin lightly.

"Hi," she said to both of them.

"So, I was thinking Charley for a name. Charley Marquez."

"No, something short." Not that she had been thinking about it, but sometimes late at night when sleep wouldn't come fast enough, she'd tossed around a couple of ideas. "No, sorry. You decide."

"We'll decide together."

Sitting up more in bed, she winced at the pull of her sutures. "You name him, Captain. Name him whatever you want. Charley."

Running a light finger down his face, his tiny head turned toward her touch. She pulled away from the soft skin and held her hand in a fist to stop herself from doing it again. A lump started forming in her throat.

"You went through all the work, and you'll have to yell at him every day for years. Better pick something you like."

"I won't be there, Holden. I was always planning to give him to you after he was born. To keep him safe." She looked away from the baby who deserved more than she could give him.

"We'll keep him safe together," Holden said with assurance. His excitement was almost catching...almost.

Dylan shook her head. "I don't want children. I never have."

"That was until we had a kid, Dylan. You can't just walk away. He needs you right now." He laid the baby down on her lap and started to open the blanket.

"He doesn't need me. There's...there's nothing I have that he can't get elsewhere." She argued, unable to look away from what he was revealing as a small hand snaked out and shot into the air.

"Food." Holden smiled softly and lifted the baby from the blanket.

"I don't have any." Her voice cracked when the baby started fussing. He wasn't too pleased with not being bound up tight.

"Yes, you do. Everyone says you have to breastfeed. It makes him... better." Holden probably knew as much as she did about babies.

Wide-eyed, she hesitantly took the baby, then looked back at Holden in alarm. "I don't know how."

His little body was hot and light. She had never held a baby this new before, or at least one that she didn't have to hand off to post-delivery. *Support the head,* her mind was chanting as she looked at him. Her perfect son.

"He does." Holden was watching her hold the baby; could he tell she had no idea what she was doing? She was in no way prepared for a baby.

"Really, Captain? You think that all you have to do is put a baby near a breast, and he'll know exactly what to do?" she demanded, not believing anything he said.

"It's Holden. And give it a try." He pulled at her gown, which was basically a blanket.

Just to prove him wrong and to establish that he was not the one with all the answers, she moved the baby toward her now-bare breast. Instantly, their son bit down on her nipple so hard it would have hurt if he had any teeth.

She was torn between amazement that her little guy was a genius or pissed that he got his brains from his father. His smug, smug father.

CHAPTER 18

His kid was definitely on his side! After a quick Internet search and one awkward video, he knew how to help his son win over his mom. Not that Dylan was heartless, but she was stubborn as hell.

The woman he was in love with wasn't even conscious yet when the head nurse had told him a social worker was coming to take the baby away. It seemed Dylan had already decided not to raise their baby. Though relieved she was handing their baby over to him, Holden knew he wasn't going to let her go that easily again.

It was going to take everything in him and their son to get her stay and be a part of their lives. No matter what she had made herself believe over the years, the woman who had saved hundreds of lives was in no way capable of abusing a child. Especially a child she loved.

He had to convince her of that, to show her she deserved to be in the baby's life…and in Holden's life. He had to show her that she was more than a doctor—she was a woman.

His first step had been to not fight with her, but he knew she had reasons for her actions and believed in them deeply. Holden felt that those reasons were stupid, but had learned in Afghanistan that yelling only caused her to get more defensive.

What he needed to do was romance her and show her what she

wanted, not simply tell her. He wanted her, and he was going to do his damnedest to get her.

"See, he knows. Smart like his mom." He touched his son's hand, and it instantly grabbed on to his finger, then slammed it into his mom's breast.

"Nature. He's just surviving," she mumbled.

"Admit it, Dyl. Our baby is a genius." He grinned at her. Her eyes were on the tiny hand holding Holden's finger against her breast.

"Let's just say he's above average for now. This might end up being his biggest accomplishment."

"I was a whole lot older than him before I got a nipple in my mouth." He watched the little mouth attaching to the breast he so enjoyed.

"You're not actually talking about sex now, are you?" She grinned.

"Of course not," he lied. "How about Todd?"

"No, Elissa's married to a Todd."

"Tony?"

"No."

"Thurston, like on *Gilligan's Island*."

"No. Must it start with a T?"

"Andrew?"

"No."

"Brett?"

"Are we going to do the entire alphabet?"

"Apparently. Carl?"

Dylan sighed. "No."

"Anyone you want to name him after? Grandpa? Dad? The best uncle you ever had?"

"Nope. I never knew any of my grandpas, and no uncles to speak of." He didn't point out that she skipped over her dad. Was it because there wasn't one, or worse?

"Okay, what about Mitch? I bet that one is fun to yell every day."

"No."

"Jack?"

"It just doesn't feel right. Are you even looking at him?" she demanded.

He looked closely at the baby, who was now on the other breast, just as happy to drink there. "Max."

"Tim, he looks like a Tim," she said, the first name she had said.

"Timothy it is."

"No, just Tim. Tim Marquez."

"Is he going to have your last name or mine?" he joked with her.

"Yours, of course. You pick the middle name." She didn't joke about it.

"Tim Jesse Marquez." He stated with a flourish.

Dylan shook her head. "No, not my father's name. Anything else." Her hand stilled on the baby's head as she said it. He could see the tension rising in her. "Here, he's done. Take him."

She pushed the baby away so fast the kid made a popping sound as her nipple left his mouth. The baby hadn't gotten the message that lunch was over and started to cry. Holden got up and started trying to sooth the baby as Dylan looked away, biting her lip.

A nurse rushed in as he was calming the baby. She was short and made busy work of checking Dylan over, not even noticing the tension in the room. Once the mother had been completely checked over, the nurse grabbed the baby from him and re-wrapped him in the blanket.

"Have you picked a name yet?" she asked as his baby once again became a burrito.

"Tim. His name is Tim Dylan."

"Well, Tim, hello there," she said to the baby, picking him up and giving him right to Dylan. She didn't even notice that Dylan didn't want the baby at that moment, but since the nurse was handing him off, she took him reluctantly.

"Next time I come in, we can make it official." She smiled at them both, then hurried out of the room.

Once the nurse had cleared the door, Dylan hissed at Holden, "Take him away from me."

Happily snatching him up from her, Holden cuddled the baby close to him. He paced the room, letting her stew in her anger or pain, whichever it was. It had been there a long time, and she'd need a little time to get over it.

When she finally spoke, she said, "We might as well get the papers signed so you can get home. Get ready."

"What papers?" He stopped walking. Her eyes were on the ceiling —she couldn't even look at him.

"I'm giving up my rights to him, so you can take him home whenever they release him." She was doing it again, pushing everyone away who could possibly love her.

Holden just stared at her for a moment before saying, "You can't."

"I already have the papers drawn up. It'll only take a few minutes."

"But Tim's breastfeeding. You can't just cold turkey that."

"It was only once; it probably doesn't count."

"Come on, Dylan. You know as well as I do that it counts." He tried to calm himself. All he wanted to do was yell at her and tell her how stupid she was being about this. Instead, he took a few calming breaths. "Don't you have a few weeks off after you have the baby, whether you take him home or not? Recovery time?"

"I guess. I was going to try to go back within a few days, but I haven't scheduled any surgeries." She admitted her plan to just push, push, push until she broke again. Hiding her pain in work as always.

"I think you should stay with Tim and me for a few weeks to recover with some help from us. No commitment, just hanging with two guys who know how to have fun." He knew once she spent a few hours with the baby and let her guard down, she would love him.

Dylan's eyes drifted to her lap. "I don't know, I don't know anything about babies."

"I don't either, but Tim will teach us."

"I would do better at the apartment, then get back to work."

"I know you have six weeks. Give us six weeks, and we will take care of you."

"And what do you get for these six weeks?"

"Free lunch, for starters. You supply this guy with beverages, and we give you anything you want."

"I don't know."

"Just give it a try, okay? Then you'll know he's being taken care of when you leave." He hated saying the words, but he had to give her an out before she would agree to anything.

"How about a week, then see how it's going?" Her eyes were back on the baby, and Holden could see the tension leaving her body as she worked out the plan in her mind.

"Works for me," he agreed. It was one step, one baby step in the right direction.

"How's your back?" she asked, fingers lightly touching the baby's blanket.

"Some pain, but not bad anymore. Thank you for working on me."

"You were on my table, I couldn't not."

"What do you do here?" he asked, because though he knew she was on staff, Mara hadn't told him.

"Surgical. All planned and routine. Oddly, it's not the routine I'm used to at all. What are you doing? I thought you'd be out."

"Recruiting. I'm kind of enjoying it, actually. Not the adrenaline rush I'm used to either."

"I hear change is good…relaxing."

"Have you called Elissa and told her the baby was here? I bet she's excited."

"I haven't talked to her since I left. She's back to her real life, so no need to talk to me." Another person cut from her life, so she didn't get attached.

"How about you rest, and we'll go tell the nurses how they're doing things the wrong way?" He grinned at her because he could tell she was exhausted, as if she had just come off a thirty-six-hour shift.

Without waiting for the argument that "she was not tired," he took the baby from the room, earning him another scolding from the nurse in charge. But he wasn't dragging a bed around with him because he wasn't putting his son down in it. He was still basking in the idea that not only did he have a son, but it was with Dylan.

CHAPTER 19

WHEN DYLAN OPENED HER EYES, the world outside her window was dark. She didn't know how long she had slept, but it hadn't been enough. What had woken her, she didn't know, but maybe it had something to do with the odd pain in her breasts?

Looking at the machine beside her, she remembered she had the baby, but the delivery hadn't gone as planned. And somehow, she had agreed to stay with Holden and help with the baby for a week, possibly more.

Sitting up a little, she looked around the room, noticing Holden was still there. His head was flopped to the side as his body slumped in an uncomfortable chair, sound asleep. As far as she could tell, the baby wasn't in the room.

Tim… He was named Tim. That was what she had been calling the little thing since the first moment she knew about him. *Trust in me,* she had promised him, telling him that she would take care of him until she could hand him off. It was supposed to be without them meeting again. A social worker was supposed to take him away and give him to Holden. He wasn't supposed to be there when she woke up from surgery.

Or sitting in the chair beside her bed, sleeping.

She didn't know what he was planning, but he was planning *something*. When he didn't yell, shout, or ask questions, she knew he was romancing her, or whatever it was considered now.

If the shoe had been on the other foot, she would have railed him for hours, mostly not letting him explain anything because she was so busy yelling. But instead, he had taken to their son, no questions asked. Holden treated their baby with a love and tenderness she knew he would, reinforcing her decision to leave Tim with him.

"Tim was getting a little hungry." A nurse came in, carrying the bundle in her arms.

Handing him off, she proceeded to leave the room immediately, like she had done this more than once before. Don't they know that this was nothing she had ever even thought about?

As Holden said, Tim knew. Within moments, his lips clamped down on her nipple as if he had been starving. In the dark silence of the room, he made little sounds as he ate. His dark hair was soft against her hand, resembling her hair. At first, she had thought he looked just like Holden, but now she could see herself in him. Her hair, her nose, maybe even her eyes one day.

Maybe he looked just like her, but she had no baby pictures of herself, so she would never know. It was the first time since she walked away from her life that she wanted to know more about herself. Had she been a good baby? A naughty toddler? When was the first time her mom thought she was lacking? How old was she the first time her father hit her?

When was she going to turn into the monster that was lurking inside her? When would Tim see it for the first time? How old would he be when Holden took him away from her?

Dylan wiped the tear from the baby's face, only for it to be replaced by another falling from her eyes. One week, that was all she was giving him. Then he would have nothing but good memories of his mom. Or none at all, which was better for everyone involved.

～

IT WAS the sixth time she had fed him because he kept falling asleep before he was done and would be hungry again quickly. The nurse said it happened a lot, and he would grow out of it. Apparently, living was hard on a new person.

Dylan felt it was an annoying, time-sucking thing. All she wanted to do was sleep for four hours straight. Hell, she'd take two hours at this point.

Holden was having no issue with the entire process; he got a good nights' sleep and didn't have to feed the baby every two hours. His life was fucking *perfect*.

"OMG! Jake told me everything. I'm so glad I'm a pushy wife!" A tall, auburn-haired woman in scrubs rushed into the room, dropped a bag on the floor, and hugged Holden. Based on her expression, it seemed like the woman's excitement was just as surprising to him. Letting him go, she turned to Dylan. "Let me see him. It's a him, right? I cannot believe this. If you need anything, I have it all! I mean it *all*. Liam, my youngest, is three, so we kept everything. We're planning to have another one day, but not yet. I've got everything from crib to clothes. All yours, if you want it." She paused for a breath, then asked, "Can I hold him?"

Holden smiled at the woman. "Dylan, this is Mara David. I work with her husband, Jake. Mara works in the ER and saw you come through yesterday. She's how I found you."

Dylan handed the baby off because Mara was going to take him anyway. "I forced Jake to tell me about the big romance, and how many girl-Dylans are there your age? Or Dylan Marquez's? I mean the J in the front threw me, but I decided to call Holden, anyway."

The woman pulled the baby close to her and smelled him. "Babies smell great. I can babysit anytime! Well, when I am not working, that is. Did you name him?"

"Tim," Holden provided.

"Timmy, I love it."

"Just Tim," Dylan stated, then hated herself. The woman wasn't doing anything wrong.

"Just Tim then. He looks like a Tim. Mine are Luke and Liam, but we want a girl. One day, we have time. Are you two going to have more?" Again, the auburn smelled the baby as she bounced him in her arms.

"Not there yet," Holden said for them. They were miles away from there; centuries away from that talk.

"Well, I mean it about the baby stuff. It's just in the garage. I'll have Jake get some stuff out after work. Maybe even take it to your place. We have it all ready. I mean, the last thing you need to do when you get out of here is put together a crib. Or are you moving in with Dylan? Oh, what am I thinking, just because Holden has nothing doesn't mean Dylan doesn't."

"I don't," she said quickly, "have anything…that is."

"Have Jake give me a call, and I can tell him where to put things," Holden said as the woman smiled bigger than she had before.

"I will, and I have a gift for the mom. So, everyone always gets the baby something, but the mom has needs too! P.S. by the second one, there are way fewer gifts." With one hand on the kid, like the expert she was, she grabbed the bag from the floor and handed it to her. "I went a little crazy, but it happens."

Dylan looked into the bag and pulled out three pairs of yoga pants, all in black. She wanted her to start exercising? Seemed odd.

"Thank you."

"It was the only thing I wore for six months after Luke was born. All stretchy, and they don't make you feel fat. Genius invention. And if you go out in them, people might think you just got back from the gym instead of just getting up from a nap. Bonus is if you wear them long enough, Holden will get sick of them and never encourage you to actually go to a gym." She giggled at herself.

"Thank you. They sound more comfortable then fatigues," she said, but doubted it, since she always wore them during her time off.

"God, yes! You're going to want to throw all your fatigues out, except for work ones," she smiled.

"You're Army?" she asked the woman. Mara was the happiest woman she had ever met, even more bubbly than Elissa.

"Reserves, but I'm done now. But I work here, so maybe not as done as I think. Just not going back to war."

The two women talked for a while about their time there and if they had ever run into the same people, with both of them being medical. They came up with a name or two before Mara had to get to work. The younger woman reluctantly handed back the baby to his parents. Very reluctantly—she nearly cried.

At the door, she stopped and mentioned, "I'll bring a car seat for him, tomorrow. You don't have one, right?"

"I haven't even thought of it," Holden said, now holding the baby.

"I'll bring it in then," she replied and paused a beat, adding, "We're waiting before we have another one."

At that, she turned and left the room, probably crying. Dylan felt bad but had no idea what she could have done. Only handing the baby over to the woman permanently would have stopped her tears, and she might have cried then also.

"I have a feeling Jake is getting lucky tonight. She's got baby-making on the brain." Holden bounced the baby in his arms.

"How old are their kids?"

"Seven and three. She got deployed not long after both were born, and she has it in her head that if she got pregnant, she would be deployed again. Though she's retired now," he explained.

"I feel bad when people have to leave their kids. Kids need their parents." She bit her lip. Her kid didn't need her, this was completely different.

He either wasn't listening or was ignoring her because he handed her back the baby. After nearly twenty-four hours, she was getting used to him being around, both Tim and his father.

"Now it seems we don't have to go shopping for everything he needs. But if you want everything new, we can. My son doesn't need hand-me-downs."

"No, it's fine. He can sleep in any crib, I think." Her insecurities on it were starting so show.

"How about you slide over and let me sit with you, and we can watch some videos on babies. See what we're getting into." He actually pushed her across the narrow bed until he could climb in.

"This isn't working." He sighed and shifted her again until she was sitting between his legs, like their movie night so many months before.

As Holden found something to watch, she saw that Tim was almost asleep. Some research sounded good, but with Holden's heat behind her and the baby's heat in front of her, she knew she was going to fall asleep any second.

A video started with a cute young mom telling how her days go with her baby. With Holden holding her tight, she let her eyes drift shut. Safe.

~

TWENTY-FOUR HOURS LATER, she hadn't changed her mind, or at least changed her mind enough to not let Holden change it back.

Mara had been true to her word, and Tim was strapped into a car seat that looked way too big for his little body. The woman had also brought pajamas that had puppies all over them and seemed like it was supposed to fit a baby way bigger than Tim. His hands kept disappearing into the sleeves, and Holden kept pulling them out.

"I don't know if I'm ready." Dylan was eying the baby as if it was going to transform into a monster at any moment.

He pulled Tim's hand out again. "I think we have it down."

"What if he gets sick or hurt? None of that was covered in anything we watched," she argued as if she hadn't slept through anything but the first two minutes of any video they watched.

"Well, Dr. Marquez, didn't you attend years and years of school to treat someone who was sick or hurt? I know for a fact that you can sew someone up pretty well." He left the baby and turned to the insecure doctor.

As usual, her eyes were on the baby, just watching him. Holden hadn't figured out if she couldn't believe he was real or if she wouldn't let herself be trusted around him.

She shook her head. "Completely different. I mean, you're comparing apples to oranges."

Wrapping his arms around her tightly he felt her stop her shaking finally, and whispered, "You can handle anything life throws at you, even a baby."

"And only for a week."

"Or six." He kissed her nose. She was nervous for nothing. Together, they would get through this.

"One week at a time, Captain."

Slipping his hands under her ass, he lifted her off the bed and set her on her feet. Since her clothes had not survived the delivery, she was in an old blue scrub top and new yoga pants. Paired with Army-issue boots, she still made it all look cute.

"Should we stop at your place to pick up your stuff?" he asked as she went into the closet and pulled out her coat and purse.

"I guess. I'll need stuff for the week." She agreed with him as usual, but always adding her time limit on it.

Picking up the car seat, he was surprised with how heavy it was compared to the baby alone. Dylan once again shoved the blankets around him more and pulled the hat more over his ears. The hat was thin and not an outside hat that he could tell, but it was all they had.

"I think I should be carrying him. You carry the car seat."

"It's fine, Dyl." He headed out the door before she could take it from him.

"The books say not to let them spend too much time in the seat," she argued as she trailed him.

"A few minutes shouldn't matter."

"The books say it, Holden. That means it's true," she snipped.

Turning to face her, he caught her with his free arm and pulled her close. "You said my name." As he kissed her lips, he felt her relax and respond. He could feel her breathe out before he stepped back.

Turning, he headed to the elevator, and this time, she was silent as they walked. Once they were waiting for the elevator, she once again tucked the blankets around the baby. Having mastered swaddling the day before, she was a firm believer in never letting their son move again.

"Is he good?" he asked. For some reason, she needed to do it, no matter how unnecessary it was.

She pulled out her keys. "I think so. I have my car running."

"I have the base of the car seat in mine, which is also running." The elevator doors swished open for them.

Stepping in the elevator, he thought how was he going to get two cars across town and get her stuff, all without her bolting? If she got into her car without Tim or anything else, she would be gone. He would have no way to find her again.

"How about you take my truck and the baby to my place, and I'll take yours to your place and get your stuff," he stated logically—if you didn't look too close at it.

"Why can't I take my car?" she asked.

"Base is in mine." He could move it, but he wasn't going to.

"Why do you have to take my car?"

"Your apartment key is on your key ring." He pointed to it, surprised it was the same key chain her room key had been on in Afghanistan.

"But…" She backed out of the elevator, searching for an argument.

"You need to get the baby home as soon as possible; it's cold out. And you have the only supply of food for him." *Blame it on the baby,* he thought. She would do it for the baby.

"I guess, though he just ate." She did one last tuck of the blanket before heading into the chilly outdoors. Luckily, it wasn't as cold as when the ice had caused her to fall.

Within minutes, he had them situated in his truck, her with a death grip on the steering wheel, and Tim already nodding off. Holden wished he could go with them, but knowing she needed to be alone with the baby for a while, he shut the door and gave a little wave. She faked a smiled at him as she backed out of the parking spot.

He had set the GPS on the truck for home and figured she would manage to get there. Her car was a little, compact thing that would do nothing but spin when the roads were slippery.

Holden got in the driver's seat and drove to her place. Not surprisingly, it was a small, rundown apartment a few blocks from the hospital. Though far enough she had to drive, it was still short enough to make the drive almost not worth it.

A moment later, he opened the door to see the rundown, furnished apartment. It only took him a couple of minutes to pack her stuff. Every article of clothing was folded perfectly, even the socks still. She had added little to her wardrobe since he was in her room on base. Just a few shirts that were folded perfectly along with her old ones. A pair of shorts was also a new addition.

Eventually, he had all of it packed. Looking around, he saw nothing for the baby, not even the books she said she had read on her phone.

In the closet on the floor was a small box and a larger box. Opening the smaller one, he saw it was completely full of letters. He immediately knew what they were and who they were from: Janet Reed. They were all still sealed, all unread.

Dylan couldn't read them but couldn't throw them out, either. Picking out a few, he saw one from years before. Holden hesitated for a moment, then read the words she couldn't. It was signed 'Mom,' as he had suspected it would. It was a short letter asking about Jessica and telling her about Jenna. The last paragraph begged her forgiveness, wishing she could change what happened.

Shoving the opened envelop deep into the box, he put the lid back on, then turned to the larger. On top was a photo of younger Dylan and Chase, mugging for the camera. Both were in jeans and Florida T-shirts, and they were standing by the ocean.

Picking it up, he saw the box was full of keepsakes from her time with him. From a bundle of letters tied with a rubber band to the medal Holden knew his brother was rewarded after death. He dug around in the box, looking for her ring. So far, she hadn't put the necklace on again. Had she put it away for safe keeping?

Closing the box, he didn't need to be reminded that her heart belonged to his brother, and always would. But he had a child with her, so maybe somehow, she could learn to love him also.

In the kitchen, he tossed out a lot of the food he found, though there wasn't as much as he had thought she would have. It seemed she might like to eat out more than cook.

The living room was free of anything that was hers except for her e-reader. After checking the closet, he saw she had added a raincoat to her meager amount of clothes.

He tucked the jacket into the crook of his arm and caught sight of a bag in the back of the closet. It was small, and he almost missed it. Grabbing it, he looked inside, expecting mittens or a hat.

Instead, he pulled out a small gray piece of cloth. Unfolding it, he saw it was a T-shirt no bigger than the one Tim had on right now. Across the chest in white letters was 'Army.'

Without a doubt she had bought this for their baby. Even if her mind was telling her she couldn't keep the baby, her heart bought him something.

The woman had purchased less than ten items of clothing since returning to the States, and one was for their baby. She wanted him; still wanted him. She had loved him from the beginning.

He had six weeks to figure out what in her past told her she couldn't have him and Tim. Putting the bag back in the closet, Holden decided it was up to her to come and get it for the baby. It was up to her to overcome her past for Tim.

He walked back to her bedroom and tossed the jacket in her bag, along with her clothes. He gathered up what little she had in the bathroom, he knew it would all fit in a plastic carrying case, but nothing was there.

Confused, Holden glanced up at the mirror. On it, he saw a Post-it note stuck to the top corner. All it said was: Trust In Me. Running down the paper was one word in capital letters: TIM.

CHAPTER 20

Sitting in the truck in Holden's driveway, Dylan debated with herself. Did she open the door and then take the baby in, which would leave the baby alone in the truck, or did she take the baby with her to open the door, taking the baby out in the cold?

Really, there was no way to be right on this. Cold baby or abandoned baby? For a woman who had spent years making split-second decisions, she couldn't decide which was worse.

Grabbing her phone, she dialed a number she hadn't called in so long. Long enough that their friendship must be over.

It rang three times before an out of breath voice stated, "This is Elissa."

Trying not to smile at the upbeat voice, Dylan asked, "Hypothetically, is it worse to leave a baby alone than it is for one to be cold? I ask because you're in the OB department."

"Dylan Marquez, is that you? Are you calling me after eight months with a hypothetical? Not even a 'hi, how have you been?'" Elissa was laughing.

"Hi, how have you been?" she asked quickly, trying to get her to answer the question.

"Great, loving being home. Miss you sometimes. Not right now, though. Right now, I'm remembering how difficult you can be. Are in you in the States still?" No mention of her breakdown, which was good. Elissa had been the one to drag her from the operating room before she actually did damage to a patient. For that, Dylan was grateful, but wondered if the other woman thought that she was mad at her. Since she hadn't talked to her since that day, she might have come to that conclusion.

"Yep. I'm in Minneapolis at the VA, for now," she added, almost forgetting about her plan to leave in a few weeks...after Tim was settled.

"Wow, we should get together sometime. I mean, it's only a flight, right?"

"That sounds fun."

"Don't sound so excited, Doc. Okay, Minneapolis, wasn't that where Holden was from? Are you with him?" She couldn't hide the excitement.

"For right now, I am. But I'm leaving soon."

"Deployed again?"

"No, I'll be stateside for now, but this was only a temporary stop."

"But you *are* with him? Are you living with him?"

"Looks like it," she said as she looked at the little ranch house he lived at, the one she was going to be staying at for a week, or maybe two.

Elissa chuckled. "I've missed you and your dry sense of humor."

"It's not really a sense of humor, you just thought I said funny things. I didn't," she defended herself. "I *am* a doctor, after all."

"And I am a matchmaker. I should turn pro."

"Good luck with that." Now it was Dylan's turn to laugh.

"So, what did my favorite workaholic doctor do with her three months off?"

"I drove."

"Too where?" Elissa asked.

"Everywhere. I saw almost every state and a dozen national parks. Then I came back to work."

"You didn't stop and see me?"

"You weren't back yet."

"I came back not a month after you, that left two months you didn't bother to stop. I thought I was your favorite nurse?" Elissa whined a little as she spoke, though Dylan could hear the underlying hurt.

"You are my favorite nurse. The one I have now is slow and has yet to read my mind."

"But the only call I get is about a hypothetical. Okay, how long?"

"How long what?"

"How long in the cold or left alone. Time and temp matter."

"Okay, say five minutes in the cold and five left alone. Shit, that is the same… Maybe four cold, six alone. If I run, four alone."

"Holy shit, woman, where is Doctor Dylan Marquez? You know, the one who can look at a man and say whether he loses a leg or not? The one that had me time her, so she knew exactly how long it took at extract a bullet?"

"That two-minute extraction was a fluke, and we both know it." Dylan smiled at the memory. Sometimes they had fun. They shouldn't have, but did.

"Tell me what's actually happening," Elissa demanded.

"I have to get the baby inside. I can leave him in the truck and unlock and open the door and then come get him. Or just take him with me, and he'll be outside as I unlock and open the door."

"How far is the door from the truck?"

"Thirty feet, maybe twenty."

"How cold is it?"

"Forty-two degrees, or so the truck stays." She was looking at the number, but was sure it was wrong. It was cold out there.

"Are we seriously talking about this? Get out of the car and take the baby inside. It will be fine, even if it takes ten minutes."

"Okay, you're right."

"Of course, I am right—I'm an expert. Send me a picture once you're inside so I know you made it," Elissa said quickly and hung up on her.

Jumping out of the warm truck, she went to the back seat where Tim was sound asleep. Dylan tucked the surrounding blankets more tightly and unhooked him, like Mara had shown her earlier.

At nearly a run, she went for Holden's front door. Shoving the key in, she got the door open and then closed, all without waking the baby or more importantly, freezing him to death.

Dylan set the car seat down in the living room and looked around at the dozens of boxes of different sizes within. Assuming they were from Mara and Jake, she looked around the house. It was smaller, with just two bedrooms. The kitchen was little but tidy, except there was a stroller, a highchair, and another item she couldn't identify in it.

The smaller of the two bedrooms had a crib, already set up and with blankets in it. Carefully, she took Tim from his seat and laid him on his back in the crib, because he could not spend a lot of time in his car seat. All the books said that!

He didn't wake up, and she breathed a sigh of relief until she got a text.

Are you dead? Baby dead?

It was Elissa. With a grin, she took a quiet picture of Tim's sleeping face. He looked so much like Holden, again. She sent the picture to her friend after she quietly closed the door to the nursery. It was the first picture she had of him. Holden had taken many, but she hadn't. Suddenly, Dylan realized she should've since she didn't have a lot of time in his life.

Her phone rang as she looked at the boxes and wondered where to start. Answering it, she was met with an angry Elissa. "I thought you had a dog! I thought you were talking about a dog! Maybe a cat, but mostly a dog!"

"I said *baby*," she reminded her in a calm voice.

"People say 'baby' all the time when they mean 'dog!' Where did you get a baby?" her friend demanded.

"My vagina," she said simply, not wanting to explain too much when Elissa would put the pieces together for her.

"Shut the front door! I need more of an explanation than that!"

"You're a nurse, Elissa, you know where babies come from. Or do I have to tell you about sex? So, when a man and a woman—"

"You're an ass. Boy or girl?" Elissa cut her off, as she knew she would.

"Boy. His name is Tim."

"And he is Holden's? Of course he is. Do the math. He's a sand baby."

"I don't know what a sand baby is."

"Conceived in the desert. Why didn't you tell me?! Did you even know? I bet you didn't even know. Wow," Elissa sighed.

"I didn't know until I got my physical in Texas."

"And now you two are together and raising a baby. So cute."

"Actually, I'm just staying here until the baby doesn't need me, then I'm transferring somewhere else. I am not mother material."

"Ha! Do you know when that baby won't need you? When he gets married, and sometimes not even then!"

"Six weeks, tops. Then I go back to work. Me and kids don't get along."

"Why won't you let yourself become attached?"

Dylan shook her head. "You don't know what you're talking about."

"Yes, I do. You keep everyone at a far enough distance that they don't become a part of you. But it's already too late this time. This kid is like your arm—you can't live without him."

"I have amputated many an arm in my day," Dylan quipped.

"But nobody laid down on your table and demand it be done; it was never their choice. Tim is a part of you forever, even if you walk out the door right now. A part of you will always be thinking about him."

"Shut up."

"*You* shut up. And call me again—I still like to talk to you." Elissa hung up on her, leaving her alone with her thoughts.

Elissa was right, as always, Tim had been her main thought since she found out about him. She had done everything for him; nothing hadn't been for the baby she'd been carrying. He was her everything, even if he deserved better than her.

Because Elissa didn't know about her past, she couldn't see how bad she was for her son. Nothing she had done in the past twenty years would make up for who she had been. That person was still somewhere inside her, hiding.

Ignoring the boxes, she went into the bathroom. She was going to take a quick shower before Holden came because after three days, she needed one desperately.

It wasn't that there wasn't a bathroom attached to her room, but the thought of taking a shower with Holden just feet from her did something to her stomach. But with him gone, she could get it done, all without taking him in there with her.

CHAPTER 21

WALKING INTO HIS HOUSE, he instantly thought she had left. At first, he couldn't see Dylan or anything she'd had with her. The crying baby was another indication that she wasn't there.

Before he could get to the spare bedroom-turned-nursery, Dylan came out cuddling the crying baby. The sight took his breath away instantly. She was whispering promises to him as she swayed back and forth, and she was mostly naked in only a pair of white panties.

Her hair was still wet from what he assumed was a shower, and her body was nicely pink, proving it was a hot one. The baby's dark hair was a sharp contrast to her white skin. Her eyes locked with his, but she gave no comment about mostly naked in front of him.

It had been months since he last saw her this way, close to it many times in the hospital, but that was different. Now here she was, in the place he had fantasied about her so many times. Okay, minus the baby.

"Where can I feed him?" she asked since the baby had also noticed his lunch was easily accessible and trying his damnedest to get at it before his mother was ready.

"Anywhere," he answered. He didn't care, as long as he got to watch.

"I need to find a spot. The books say to use the same location." She started looking around the house. She had read two books on her phone about babies, apparently turning her into an expert. Or perhaps the books gave her the rules she had so desperately needed.

"Couch?" he offered.

"No, doesn't feel right."

"Bed?" He had no idea where a "good location" would be.

"No, that'll disturb you at night." As if seeing her feed their child wasn't his favorite thing to watch these days.

He gestured at his favorite recliner. "Chair?"

"I don't know about the chair." She eyed it suspiciously as the baby found his mark.

"Well, you can't just stand there," he teased, then gently pushed her toward the chair. It might've looked worn out, but it was great.

Settling in, she adjusted the baby as if she'd been caring for him for months. Each had learned their duty and didn't think twice about it anymore. She pulled her legs up under her as her eyes stayed on the baby. With her one-handed hold on him, she took his little hand in hers and brought it to her mouth and kissed it.

"Are you cold?" he asked. Holden couldn't take his eyes off of her. Just when he thought he loved her, she did something totally amazing, and he loved her more.

"No, I was in the shower." She didn't have to say, he guessed it already.

"Feeling better?" he knew he had to stop ogling her, so he grabbed a box and opened it.

"Yes, except now I'm tired again. Or still. Or more. I thought I knew the stages of being tired, but this is a whole new level." She kissed the little hand again.

"After he's done, you can sleep. I'll organize this stuff," he said, motioning to the boxes.

"The house might be too small for all this stuff." She looked around at it skeptically.

"We'll squeeze as much of it in as we can. I got your stuff too. There's room in the bedroom for it." It was only after renting the house that he realized how little he actually owned after thirty years.

"Okay." She burped the baby against her naked shoulder as if her stuff didn't matter. "I called Elissa."

"How is she? Loving being home? Did she know you were pregnant?" He had thought Dylan had cut her out already, as she did with anyone she got too close to.

"Happy still. I forgot to ask about the kids and Todd." She put the baby on her other breast. "I hadn't told anyone. My CO and my supervisor, but nobody else."

Again, she completely absorbed herself in feeding the baby by looking at him and touching him. He let it go—she had to work it out in her mind. She had to realize she wanted people close to her.

Opening the box, he started to pull out blankets, mostly in shades of blue, but sometimes another color showed up. Pulling out the top one, he laid it over Dylan and Tim.

The scowl she shot him as she pushed it off them was a surprise. "Everything has to be washed, Captain. *Everything.*"

Groaning, not because washing everything was going to take forever, but because she was back to using "Captain" again. He couldn't decide if it was a reflex or a way to keep them distant. He assumed the latter.

"It's Holden, okay? I'll start washing things. But he only has one outfit and a nasty habit of getting poop everywhere." He gestured at his boy.

"Better snap to it then," she quipped as she unfolded herself from the chair. "I'll put him in his crib and take a nap."

She started yawning, so he let her go—she needed sleep. He wished he could feed his son, but there was no way he was going to let her see she wasn't needed. Because that was the day she would be gone.

CHAPTER 22

IT HAD BEEN over a week since they'd brought the baby home. Slowly, they had put everything away and made some much-needed room in the house, but the additional items that the baby needed were taking up a *lot* of space.

His first day back at work, he had started looking for a new place for the three of them. Something close to the VA since she liked to be close to work and something big enough for everything Tim would ever need. Though he hadn't talked to her about it, and he only had his income on the application, he was still able to look at nice-sized places.

He was back to work the day after Dylan moved in, mostly so she was alone with the baby. That decision was something she hadn't been happy about, but he had come up with enough excuses about babysitting and job duties that she stopped questioning it.

To his delight, she was loving being a mom, though she would never admit it. Every day when he got home there were stories of what Tim had been up to that day. A play-by-play of the day was reported in full detail, and then she would take a nap for a few hours while he took care of the baby.

So far, she hadn't said a word about leaving again, though he knew she was still thinking about it. Not that he would bring it up—no way was he reminding her of that decision. She actually hadn't said anything about any of her decisions, from where she'd been when she was on leave to why she was so willing to walk away from her son. What could possibly have happened for her to even think she could do that?

Dylan was happy to sleep in his arms at night, not once requesting he sleep on the couch or with just her. It wasn't like anything was happening between them. Though sometimes, Holden just watched her sleep, loving how at peace she looked in slumber.

Since it was a Friday and quiet at the recruitment office, Jake had sent him home early. It was his way of thanking Holden for all the times Holden had let him go home when Mara was home over the last few months.

Holden loved the idea of rushing home to watch Dylan be a mother or holding his son. She was a better mother than she'd ever let on that she could be. Her heart was in that baby pretty deep.

But he knew he had another thing to do that Dylan couldn't help him with. He had to tell his parents, about both the baby and Dylan.

After pulling into the driveway, he saw his mom was raking leaves while his dad sat on the deck watching her. It was the same way it had been his entire life: Mom was busy, and Dad lived on the fact that he had a job.

Seeing Holden getting out of the truck, his mom straightened and smiled at him. He hadn't called, and was happy that they were both home, making all this a lot easier.

"I am glad you two are home," he said, giving his mom a hug. His mom didn't touch his back as she put her arms around him.

"Of course we're here, where else would we be?" his dad asked from the deck, not moving.

"Maybe headed to Roark and Karin's place?" he answered, knowing his parents didn't go out there much. Dad usually had some issues with his boys, and Roark retired from the Navy too early.

"Nope, just putzing around here." His mom looked back at the yard.

"Good, I stopped by because I wanted to tell you in person."

His dad sat up straighter. "Tell us what?"

"While I was still in Afghanistan, I ran into Dylan," he began, waiting for their reactions.

"Dylan who?" his mom asked with a questioning look in her eyes.

"Sorry, I mean Jessica. Jessica Dylannski Marquez. Chase's wife." He hated saying the words, that his brother had some claim to her, ever after all these years.

His mom's eyebrows went up in surprise. "Is she still in the Army? I would have assumed she would have found someone else to marry by now."

"She has twenty years in, Mom, and she's a doctor now. She not only took the bullet from my leg, but fixed my back before I was sent to Germany." He hoped that would help them understand what a great person she was.

"I'm sure she's married. Probably a few times over by now. Poor Chase." His mom sighed and shook her head.

"She's *not* remarried," he hissed at his parents, wishing he didn't have to defend the love of his brother's life…and his.

"She will, her kind always does." His dad chuckled a little, as if he knew anything about her.

"Yes, Dad, I hope to God she does marry someone—me. And if you're going to treat her like you did when she was married to Chase, you won't see me much either." He took a step back from them, hating that they were so cruel to one person.

"Jesus, boy, she's nearly a decade older than you! You can get any hot little thing you want!"

"I want her. If you can't accept that, then I'll be on my way," he said, turning to leave.

"Holden, wait," his mother called after him.

He paused for a moment. "What?"

"Is she still in Afghanistan?"

"No, she's living with me and works for the VA now. She's an amazing surgeon."

"Is that what you came out here to tell us? That you're wasting your life just like your brother did on that woman?" his dad chided, shaking his head.

"No, I actually stopped by to tell you that Dylan and I have a son.

He's a week old, and his name is Tim. But you will *never* see him until you're willing to accept Dylan and treat her the way she deserves."

"A baby," his mom called after him. "Do you have pictures?"

"He looks like his mother, so I assume you don't care." He climbed into his truck.

Thinking that your parents would disapprove of your life was different from them saying it. Every major choice in his life had disappointed his parents—this was just another drop in the bucket, but this was also one where he would walk away from them before he ever gave in.

Dylan was his life now, he just had to get her to realize it.

Pulling into his own driveway twenty minutes later, he knew it was still earlier than he usually came home, but now he was excited to see how her day had gone and how Tim was.

"Dylan, I'm home," he called out as he stepped through the door, shrugging out of his jacket and hanging it up.

He was disappointed when she didn't respond back. Usually, she called out her location or said, "Daddy's home!" Then he would find her in the house a drop a kiss on her forehead or cheek. So far, he hadn't pushed her about anything except a goodnight kiss, which she happily gave him.

Taking off his shoes, he still didn't hear a response from her. In fact, the house was eerily quiet. Usually, she was busy with something, from doing laundry to reading in the living room when he came home.

Tossing his shoes aside, he went to Tim's room and found it empty. The crib had a tiny set of pajamas in the middle of it, but no baby. The rest of the room was spotless, as it always was. Dylan was a fastidious cleaner.

Holden peeled off his work shirt as he left the baby's room, then found the two people who were most important to him in his and Dylan's bed. The baby was lying on his back in the middle of the bed, his hands raised above his head.

Dylan was lying on her side in the leggings she constantly wore now and an old gray Army shirt. One of her arms was nested under the pillow, and the other hand was stretched out and resting on Tim's stomach.

After a week, he had never caught her sleeping with the baby. She had always been up, and if he was home, he had the baby. He looked at the two of them now, facing each other.

Tossing his shirt on the dresser, he quietly climbed onto the bed and laid on his side, watching them sleep. Mostly his eyes were on the woman, the one who thought she couldn't be trusted around kids.

Since coming home from the hospital, he hadn't noticed her wearing her wedding ring, neither on a chain nor on her finger. In fact, she hadn't worn any jewelry at all.

The only exception was her hair. She rarely braided it here, almost always leaving it free and hanging down her back.

Holden laced his fingers through hers over the baby's belly and shut his eyes, enjoying the quiet time with his family.

CHAPTER 23

AFTER HANGING UP ON ELISSA, Dylan wondered how she would have made it this far without her friend's advice. Sadly, nearly every day, she would call the woman about something or other. Today it had been about Tim's sudden need to be held or cuddled. Most days, he was content to lie on the floor, but not today.

Elissa had assured her that it was normal and just a thing for today. Dylan had returned the favor, letting her friend rant about work for a while. Back in the OB, Elissa was bored. The excitement of Afghanistan had gotten to her, and she was no longer happy just being an OB nurse.

So far, she wasn't bored enough to move to the ER, which was Dylan's suggestion, but she knew with time, the woman would eventually have to change jobs and offered to give her recommendations if needed.

Sadly, Dylan was going to be facing the same thing when she got back to the VA, even if she was in the surgical department. She, too, had been bored before Tim had been born, but since she'd been pregnant, she had little options.

Now with the baby in her arms, options opened before her, but she didn't want to think about them. After four weeks, Tim wasn't nearly ready to be without her—he was still dependent on her for food, and she wasn't aware if Holden had been looking for childcare yet.

Which was something he needed to do, and fast. In two weeks, no matter what, she was going to be back at work. Whether she still lived with Holden or not, she couldn't be there all day with the baby.

Maybe that was why Tim was so clingy today—he knew she was thinking about leaving. Today she had called her boss at the VA and had gotten back on the schedule. Her time with Holden and their son was nearly over. While she was pregnant, she had wanted to leave as soon as she could, but knew Tim still needed her now.

All week during their phone calls, Elissa had dropped hints on how to be a working mom. Everything she said made sense and seemed easy to do. Until Dylan remembered that once she started working she would be back in her apartment and Tim would be with Holden still.

Based on her reading, she could start transitioning him to a bottle at any moment. They were all washed and ready to go with a container of formula sitting right next to it. That way, Holden wouldn't need her at all.

In two weeks, not only would she have to go back to work, but any excuse to stay with Holden would also be over. He could do most of the work on his own.

Then what would her excuse be to see her son, when she didn't really have one? Whether she was across town or back in the desert, it wouldn't matter. It wouldn't take them long for them to forget her.

She set the baby in his bouncing thing, then checked him again for a temperature or anything that might be irritating him. This was the third time she had checked, and so far, had found nothing.

His blue eyes followed her around, making sure she didn't leave him. Today he was determined to keep her with him constantly.

With a sigh, Dylan gathered him up again and held him close, admitting that maybe she needed him close to her also. Maybe it wasn't all him.

The doorbell suddenly rang, causing the both of them to jump. She hurried over to answer the door, wondering who it could be. It wasn't every day that someone came over, but sometimes Mara came before work, or the UPS guy brought something Holden had ordered. Most of the time, it was something for Tim.

Swinging the door open, she looked straight into eyes that were so much like Holden's, except they belonged to his mother. They were not happy or mad, just worried, and Dylan's stomach instantly sank.

"Is Holden home?" she asked tentatively, looking at the baby.

"Uh, he's at work," Dylan told her, but his mother would know that. His schedule was mostly eight to five and hadn't changed in a while.

"Oh, I was wanting to talk to him." Donna Marquez's eyes were still glued to the back of the little boy who was scrunched up on Dylan's chest.

"You can call him." She turned away from the door, protecting her little guy from her.

Leaving the woman standing just outside the open door, Dylan went into the house and tried to ignore the fact that the woman didn't leave. Donna just stood there in the open door watching her. Dylan for her part ignored that she was supposed to be a good hostess and let her in.

"Holden said his name was Tim. Is it just Tim or Timothy?"

"Just Tim," she answered.

"Holden said we can't see him until we learn to treat you better, so I want to apologize right now for all the mean things I said to you."

"I don't care how your treat me, Mrs. Marquez—I never have. All I ever cared about was how you treated Chase, and now Holden. If you can't respect your sons, you can't respect *my* son."

"I was always proud of my children in whatever they did. Maybe I wasn't very good at showing them that, but it is true."

"Maybe you should make a point of telling them sometimes, not just letting them wonder."

"I am going to try harder from now on. Holden said you were some kind of doctor." Donna Marquez still was outside, but the screen door was now open.

"A surgeon, actually. I sewed up Holden's back before he came home."

"Thank you for that, and his leg. He said you fixed that also."

"Yes, but that was minor." If it hadn't been for his leg wound, however, Tim wouldn't be there now.

"It could have been worse, and later on, it was. His back was bad when he got here. They should have kept him longer, I told him that."

"He had no say in his recovery. The doctor treating him must have thought that he was well enough to go home to parents who could help him recover. Did you help with his recovery or hinder it?" Her arms went tighter around her own son, knowing there was nothing he could do that she wouldn't help him with in any way possible.

"I did everything they told me to do."

"I hope so. Holden needs support, not negative words about his life and the choices he made. He was a great soldier and when he was injured, he knew his life would never be the same. All he wanted to do was be a soldier—accept that and move on. You haven't been able to change it in a decade, and you aren't going to now."

"I never tried to change his mind," Donna argued, shaking her head.

"Just talked down about what he wanted to do and what he liked to do. Just like with Chase."

"Chase made some bad decisions also."

"Look, Mrs. Marquez, I am sorry I fell for your son, either of them. I didn't really mean for it to happen this time. I mean, after Chase died, I didn't think I would—hell, could—love anyone else. I had built walls to protect myself, but Holden somehow broke through them. For some reason, he wanted to."

"Maybe he saw the same thing Chase did."

"No, I think Holden sees more. Holden sees things in me I don't see. I know I should've walked away the moment Tim was born. Holden would've raised Tim and found someone better to love. But I was selfish and stayed. I know he deserves more than me, and I'm planning on leaving soon, so he can find someone better."

"You would just walk away from the baby?" Donna's eyes went immediately to the baby's back again.

"That was the plan ever since I knew I was pregnant. Holden will be a great dad, but I'm not the kind of mother Tim deserves."

"Does Holden know?"

Dylan dropped her eyes to the floor. "Yes and no. I told him right away, but I don't think he believes it."

"I don't either. You can't just walk away."

"It'll be better for everyone. You don't want me as the mother of your grandson."

"It doesn't matter what I want or not—you *are* his mother. And you always will be, whether you're here or not."

Dylan shot her a pointed look. "You would prefer I not be."

"Yes, well, I admit I'm not your biggest fan. But for some reason, I have two sons who have fallen in love with you, so maybe I'm missing something. The fact that this is the longest conversation we've ever had says something about how little I know about you."

"Maybe I never tried, either. It was easier to be a few states away and have Chase as our go-between, but at the time, I was still a little raw from my own parents' negative view of me to have someone else's do the same. Maybe if he hadn't died, we could have become closer over the years."

"Possibly, we'll never know, but I'd like to try for Holden and Tim."

"We could, but you would have to stop with the negative talk about the Army—we're both still in it, and we've both spent years devoted to it. As far as I know, your husband only survived the minimum in the Navy."

"I will if you will let us be a part of your son's life." She looked at Dylan with sincerity.

Dylan smiled and said, "I think we have a deal. Do you want to come inside and hold him? I've had to pee for an hour now."

"I would love to." She hurried over and held her arms out.

Tim's eyes went wide for a second as someone else took him from his mother, then he relaxed as Dylan excused herself.

Maybe by the time she left her son behind, he would have loving grandparents to help his father as well.

CHAPTER 24

OTHER THAN AS the mother of his baby, Dylan was sure Holden wasn't interested in her anymore. When they had had their great romance in the desert, she had been flattered that he had focused on her. At first she had thought to herself he wasn't interested in her, he was interested in a woman, she was that. But eventually, he made her believe that he was interested in her for herself, that she was special.

But since Tim's birth, he had kept his distance. There were a few hugs and kisses, but rarely on the lips, and never the toe-curling, body-melting kisses she had come to expect from the man. Even in bed, the one they shared, he kept his distance.

After a month, they were just roommates with a baby. Soon, they wouldn't even be that.

Pushing her emotions back deep inside where they belonged, she pulled out the container of formula and read it again. She'd done this over a dozen times since Donna had visited two days before, but so far, she hadn't opened the container. She simply read how it was going to work and wondered if Tim would like it.

Holden called out from the door like he always did, and Dylan slammed the container back in the cabinet, as if catching her with it would be a bad thing. In fact, she didn't know if he would be happy that she was gearing Tim up for her departure or mad she that was making decisions without him.

She looked at the clock as the cabinet door slammed shut and frowned. "What are you doing home so early?"

He came through the kitchen door and grinned at them. "I took off early to go look at a house, something bigger for us."

His words made her heart do a little flip, until she realized "us" didn't necessarily mean her, just Tim and him. "How was it?"

How could she tell him she wanted to see where their son was going to be raised? It wasn't her place to agree or disagree, but she wanted to know where he would be sleeping and eating and playing.

"I came to get you, so we could look together," he said. She felt his eyes on her, but she was looking at the baby—her emotions were too much today.

"You picked a good time; he just ate and is ready for an adventure." She handed him the baby.

"Great! I was hoping it was a good time. It's just a few miles away and shouldn't take long. I saw that they were having an open house today, and I thought we could go take a look." He followed her from the kitchen into the living room with Tim.

"Maybe I can take a nap while you two are gone." She grabbed the blue blanket from the couch and folded it. It was dirty and needed to be washed, but she needed something to do.

He was bouncing Tim in his arms but stopped and looked at her. "I thought we could go together."

"I don't want to intrude, Captain." Even to her, the words sounded hollow.

She saw his jaw clenching for a moment before he said, "You don't at least want to see where he'll be living? You don't care?"

Her eyes pleaded with him. "Of course, I care, Holden. But it's your decision." A decision that said he was starting his life without her.

"Then get your coat—we're looking at a house. *Together*." His words held an edge she usually didn't hear from him. Not once since they'd gotten back together had they fought, argued, or even really talked.

For a while, she just watched him put Tim in his car seat with ease.

It was something she wasn't overly familiar with since she rarely went anywhere. Mostly, she was too tired to even think about going places, not that she even knew where to go.

Dylan went back in the bedroom, grabbed a sweatshirt, and threw it over the T-shirt she always wore, Army-issue. For the most part, she hadn't brought much with her since she felt like this was a mission—a mission to ensure her son was loved by his father. Though she knew Holden would love Tim until the end of time, she hated knowing she wouldn't get to see it.

Dylan looked at her boots and frowned—they didn't go with her leggings. Turning back to change into her fatigues, Holden grabbed her arm and handed her a pair of no-longer-white tennis shoes. He must've grabbed them that first day, and she had never noticed.

Mumbling a thanks, she slipped them on as he watched since he was already dressed and had Tim in his carrier. Once the shoes were on, he pushed her out the door and into the waiting sunshine. All the snow had vanished; even the grass had started to grow while she'd been inside spending every moment she could with her son. While she still could.

The ten-minute drive went quickly, and Tim was silent the entire time, probably excited to be in a car again. Hopefully, he was getting used to it because once she went back to work, he would be traveling a lot more.

The house that Holden had found was beautiful, it even had a picket fence out front to keep Tim from playing in the street, Holden told her. The two stories held four bedrooms and three bathrooms, way more than the two of them would need.

Inside, the entire house smelled of apple pie, of home. After slipping booties on their feet as a sign requested at the front door, Dylan started taking Tim from his chair.

"Just leave him, he's okay in there," Holden stated.

"All the books say to take him out," she argued, as she always did. Books were written for a reason.

"He's fine."

"He's been clingy today." She pushed past him into the kitchen, which was all dark wood that gleamed in the sunshine.

Instantly, she could see Tim and Holden there, Tim older at the counter and Holden making something at the stove. It was the house they needed.

As the baby squirmed in her arms, she knew this was the house he would learn to walk in. He would leave from here to go to school every day, and this would be the house he would think of as home when he was an adult. Here.

"Welcome to 506 Elmwood Drive," a voice stated from behind her.

Dylan's breath caught in her throat. She didn't have to turn around to know exactly who had said it. Pictures of her son's life faded from her mind and were replaced by ones of her life.

Years of disappointment over her not making the cheer squad to her distress over not being the perfect daughter, instantly flooded her. Since the day she had arrived in town, she knew her mother now sold real estate, but she didn't think she would be here, at the one house Holden had taken her to.

Behind her, Janet must have found Holden, who was introducing them to her. "I'm Holden Marquez, and this is Dylan, with our son, Tim."

"I'm Jan Reed, and you guys take a look around house and see what you think," her voice said brightly.

Turning, Dylan held her breath. It had been twenty years—was she even recognizable? Her mom certainly was. She still sported blond hair, now from a bottle like Dylan's had been all through high school, her natural color long gone due to age. The short style suited her, though.

Though her mother looked at her, she didn't seem to recognize her. Maybe it was due to the scar that she hadn't had the last time they saw each other, or maybe because she was no longer built like she had been before. Though Dylan was sure she hadn't recognized her, she could've picked her mother out in the middle of a busy street.

"How old is the baby?" Janet asked, her eyes on him.

Dylan held him a little closer. "A month now."

"Fun age, exhausting but fun. My oldest is nearly forty."

Was she really talking about me?!

"What does she do?" Dylan held her smirk, her mother had no idea. Or maybe she did.

"Army, like your husband." Janet turned to look where she heard him wandering around the house. Dylan picked up on the fact that her mother didn't name where, rank, or duty—the woman had no idea.

"How about your other kids?" she asked, knowing Jenna worked with her.

"My other daughter works with me, and my stepson is a police officer." Her words stopped Dylan. Who was the stepson? When she had left, her mother had been single and had trouble trusting men after an abusive first marriage.

"I didn't know you were married," she said, instantly realizing her mistake. She had known about her mom's name change before Dylan had married herself, but it had been so long ago, she had forgotten.

Thankfully, Janet didn't notice. "Yes, for seventeen years now. He's an amazing man."

"I'm happy for you." Dylan turned from her and looked out the back door at the yard. It was bigger than she'd thought it would be. Tim would love it one day.

"What's his name?" Janet had moved closer to her.

"Tim," she responded as Holden came back into the room.

"How about I hold Tim, and you two go check out the house together?" Janet offered and held out her arms to the baby.

Dylan turned away from her, stepping behind Holden. "No, thank you."

There was *no way* she would trust that woman with her son. Once in her arms, she would probably find fault in him. Something to pick at for years until he too had no confidence in himself.

With a quick glance at the confused look on Holden's face, she left the room and looked over the house. As she had expected, it was utterly gorgeous. Everything was perfect. Too perfect.

Though she hadn't gone upstairs yet, she knew they'd be happy here. Holden leaned against the fireplace mantel and asked, "What do you think?"

The smile on his face indicated that he loved it and that he also knew it was perfect. It was the place he should raise their son.

"I like it." She downplayed her love of the house, nodding slightly as she rocked Tim in her arms.

"Me too. It's perfect."

"Nothing is *perfect*, Holden. It's just a house."

"Do you think we should get it?" he asked.

"It's the first one we saw! Don't you want to look at another one?"

"Nope, this one is *the* one. I can feel it." Again, it was like he had read her mind.

Janet came through the doorway and asked, "So, how do you like it?"

"It's great. Exactly what we're looking for," Holden replied.

"It is a great house, isn't it? If you're not working with an agent, I am available to look at some more with you," Janet offered with a smile.

"I don't know if we need to look at anymore. I have to talk to the bank and see how we're going to swing it, but this one is perfect."

Dylan watched her mother flinch at the word, the same way Dylan always did. *Nothing* was perfect. "Perfect" was the word you hid behind when your husband beat you bloody regularly. "Perfect" was how you act so your kids don't get the same treatment, and failed

"With one child, maybe four bedrooms is too large of a house," Janet stated, looking at Holden's uniform and calculating how much he could possibly make. Obviously, the numbers were not adding up.

"No, I think we need the space. Tim could use two himself right now, right Dylan?" he chuckled, but neither of the women joined in.

"What she means, Holden, is that you probably cannot afford this house." Dylan shifted Tim in her arms, he was a dead weight when he slept.

"I-I'm sure you are doing fine financially," Janet stammered, color rising in her cheeks.

"No, you don't. You think we're a cute little family who can't afford half this house. How much is it?" Dylan asked, because she hadn't asked before. She'd been told where to live for twenty years now, and there was rarely a cost to her.

Her mother's answer shocked her a little, mostly because Dylan really didn't know how much houses cost. The number was actually less than she had in her bank account right now. Her reaction was clearly visible since her mother quickly added, "Don't worry, I can find you something just as nice in your price range. Just contact the bank and see what it is. You can trust in me."

"Why would I trust you?" Dylan spit at her, turned, and marched past Holden who tried to grab her, but missed. Leaving the house with her son in her arms and the booties still on her feet, she couldn't stand another moment in that house with her mother.

Stopping at the truck, she knew she looked like an idiot, but she climbed in anyway. From the front seat, she watched Janet and Holden talking on the porch. Were they talking about her? Was he telling her that she was a doctor, that they could afford the house even if it didn't seem like it?

Years before, when she had told her mom she wanted to be a nurse, not even admitting then that she had wanted to be more than that, they'd been living in a little apartment away from the "perfect house" with all its secrets. Jenna was away with friends, like usual. She was two years younger than Dylan, but she was popular and sporty.

"So, Jess, what do *you* want to be when you grow up?" Her mom loved asking that question. She asked both her daughters it all the time.

"I was thinking a nurse, or maybe a doctor." She had been taking science classes for years and loved them.

Her mom looked up from the salad she was making and tilted her head to the side, obviously confused by her answer. When it was just the two of them, her mother made salad. Dylan's weight was always a problem. With a chuckle, Janet said, "I can't see you as a nurse, Jess. You're just not calm enough, and you hate blood."

So, maybe at the time she wasn't calm, but she was only seventeen! It was really her mother who'd hated the sight of blood—Dylan had grown used to it by growing up in a "perfect" house.

When she had told the recruiter her same dream six months later, he had her tested for medical aptitude and steered her toward being a doctor. A stranger saw that Dylan could be more than her own mother did, but then again, her mother wasn't her biggest cheerleader, she was Jenna's.

Holden suddenly opened her door, snapping her back to the present. He face was a mask of confusion as he took the baby from her and put his car seat in the base. Dylan just stared at the house, the house she wanted so badly, but not enough to go through her mother to get.

Holden didn't say a word as he got into the cab and drove them back to their house. When he parked and got out, he didn't say a word then either. Dylan watched him take the baby into the house, and her heart sunk. She knew he was pissed but wasn't going to yell at her.

Or maybe he wasn't pissed, she thought. *Maybe he was just indifferent.*

CHAPTER 25

HOLDEN TOOK another sip of beer, trying to get his anger settled before he talked to Dylan again. Her indifference to the house was bothering him. She said she liked it, but she only saw half of it, if that. She didn't even bother to look upstairs.

Then she made the real estate agent think he couldn't afford the house! For years he had saved most of the money he made, and he had a nice nest egg to draw from for a down payment. He knew exactly how much he could afford. The house was doable.

Could it be that *she* didn't think he could afford it? All she had to do was ask him. Or just talk to him, not tell the real estate agent he was too poor to pay for the house by himself.

It wasn't that he needed to do it himself—he wanted her there also. Not for the money, but because she was the main part of the life he wanted to live. But it was a life she didn't seem to want to be a part of, however.

Tim was waking from his nap when he heard the front door finally open, letting him know Dylan was back. When they had arrived home, she had stayed in the car. Now, he heard her walk across the living room and go into the bedroom. Holden set his beer down and got up. He knew that the baby needed to eat soon, or he'd start crying.

He found her in their bedroom, still in her sweatshirt and leggings, and still as gorgeous as ever. There were clothes on the bed, and he couldn't tell if she was putting them away or taking them out.

He walked into the room, ignoring her clothes, and handed her the baby. "Tim's waking up."

"He isn't hungry yet. Just take him and play with him a while." She tried to hand the baby back.

With a side-step, he dodged her and leaned against the wall, watching her. "What did you really think of the house?"

"It was nice. You'll be happy there." She sat down with the baby, and despite her words, lifted her shirt up to feed him.

"It's more than nice, Dylan."

"It was gorgeous, Holden, and Tim will love growing up there."

He narrowed his eyes a little. "I was thinking about a swing set in the backyard."

"He's a little young yet, but one day." She took Tim's hand and kissed it.

"I think we can get the price down a bit. It's a little high."

"I can give you the money for it, so I know that Tim is taken care of. I have the money."

"*I* have money, Dylan! I haven't spent much over the years. I don't need yours." Money would never make up for Tim's mother not being there, not loving him as she should've.

"I know you don't, but I want to make sure that Tim has everything he needs." Her words caught him off guard—the baby had never wanted for anything in his life.

It seemed that maybe Dylan was projecting onto her son what had been lacking in her own life. Could it be that the house was something Dylan had dreamed about but wouldn't let herself have?

"Maybe Jan is right, and there's something just as good at a lower price," he suggested.

"No, that was the one, and I'll pay for half. Tim will be happy there. It's the home he deserves." Her eyes were locked on the baby, a baby who would be happy any place his mom was.

"You only looked at half the house. How do you even know he'll like it?"

"I saw enough, and I'll see the rest maybe one day. I've never been that picky about where I live." She was still looking at the baby, who had nodded off in her arms.

Holden pushed off from the wall and gently took the baby from Dylan, then carried him across the hallway and laid him in his crib. Somehow, he didn't notice that he was now in his bed and not in his mom's loving arms.

Dylan was still sitting on the bed, staring at the closet door.

"You didn't think the house was too big?" Holden quizzed her. He needed to know that she liked the house.

"Maybe a little, but this one is too small. Tim has a lot of stuff and probably always will."

"The bedrooms upstairs were a little on the small side."

"Oh, but they were big enough, right?"

Holden folded his arms across his chest. "Maybe you should have gone up and looked."

"I didn't need to, really. I'm sure they're big enough."

"Maybe we need to go look again. This time, you can go upstairs."

"Just get the house or don't get the house, Captain. Do what you want." She got up and tried to push past him, but he grabbed her arm.

"Why didn't you want to see where your son would be sleeping, Dylan?" He pulled her close to him, and her eyes flashed with anger.

"*Don't,*" she hissed.

"Why didn't you go up those stairs?"

"I didn't need to see the room you would bring other women home to. I didn't need it rubbed into my face."

"Really, Dylan? What other women? I sleep with *you* every night." He pointed to the bed they'd been sharing for weeks.

"It'll be over next week. I'll go back to my place and work, and you can start finding a new mom for Tim. He deserves a good one." The anger was gone, replaced by the same hollowness she had when she closed off her emotions.

"He deserves you. *You* are the person he wants, and you're who I want in mine."

"You're not even attracted to me anymore, Captain. I was just a fling, someone you forgot about the moment you came home. If it hadn't been for Tim, I wouldn't be here. I understand that."

"In what way am I not attracted to you, Dylan? I walk around this house with an erection from morning until night! I can barely keep my hands off of you, ever." He argued, as if she hadn't noticed.

"You do a fairly good job of it," she said petulantly.

"That's because I know if I touched you, let alone kissed you, I wouldn't stop until my cock was buried in you so deep you'd have no idea where you ended and I began. But you clearly aren't ready to have sex yet, so I don't touch you because I can't trust myself around you. Not your lips when you bite them, not your neck that I know smells of lilacs in the spring, and not your breasts that I get to see almost every day as they nurture our son. The son *we* created that grew in your body, the one you loved and cared for as it happened." His free hand skimmed over her stomach and cupped her bare breast firmly.

"You never let on," she breathed out.

"What was the point? You were recovering from giving birth to our son. There was nothing I would rather see you do than that. It's hands down the sexiest thing I've ever seen," he admitted, not carrying that it made him seem weak.

"You clearly don't know what sexy is." Her lips curled into a slight smile.

"Sexy is watching you feed our son in the same spot every day. Sexy is you reading book after book on how to raise our son. Sexy is you sleeping in a bed right next to our son, keeping a hand on him and never letting anything bad happen to him. Sexy is you *right now* in those fucking pants, letting me see the ass and legs I constantly dreamt of as I lay in a hospital bed with my back ripped apart."

Her eyes went wide for a second, then drifted to the floor between them. "I don't feel very sexy."

"Then let's change that," he whispered and pulled her tight to him.

His lips claimed hers and were met with equal passion. Her hand wrapped around his neck as their lips, tongue, and teeth met in a frenzy. Lifting her up, Holden carried her to the bed he had wanted her in like this since she'd walked back into his life. Hell, since *long* before that.

CHAPTER 26

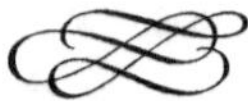

DYLAN CURSED as she glanced at the time displayed on the car's radio. Her errands had run long, too long, and she still had one more stop to make before heading home. It was her first time away from Tim since his birth, and she missed having him around.

Though she knew she really didn't have to, she had gone to the VA to make sure everything was ready for her return. Dr. Roads, head of surgery, was happy to see her back since he was taking on the extra work while she was gone. Having looked over her schedule, she knew what to expect from her return: boring, ordinary surgeries.

She wasn't even back yet and already felt bored with the work, knowing who and what was coming next. She knew she had spent too much time in Afghanistan, but she missed the fast pace of it.

After the hospital, she had stopped at her apartment, which she hadn't been to at all since Tim was born. It helped that Holden had grabbed almost everything she owned from it. Today she would grab the rest; there was no need to keep an apartment she wasn't living in.

Now that she and Holden were more than just sleeping side by side, she didn't think he would mind if she brought over the last of her stuff. After loading the two boxes into the car, she went back and grabbed a small bag she had hidden from herself in the closet. When she had first found out she was pregnant, she had quickly found herself buying an outfit for the baby.

After traveling with the outfit for months, she had hidden it in the closet in hopes of forgetting that she wanted to see it on the baby. She knew she never would. Now, she didn't have to worry.

Pulling to a stop in front of Jan and Jen's reality, she hoped that neither would be in the office today. She wasn't there for a family reunion, she was there to buy a house for her son and Holden. And maybe a little for herself, a safe place for her family, with or without her.

Taking a deep breath, she pushed into the office and was met by a smiling face, one that didn't belong to her sister or her mother. With a quick look around, she didn't notice either of them there.

"Welcome to Jan & Jen. What can I help you with, officer?" a brunette asked in a cheerful voice.

Dylan had forgotten that she was in her fatigues. They were so familiar, she forgot that they weren't the usual attire for everyone. After six weeks, she was just as comfortable in leggings, but since she was visiting the hospital, she wore the fatigues.

"I want to buy a house," she said, her plan set. Even though she knew Holden would argue with her about buying the house, she had to do it.

"Anything in particular?"

"506 Elmwood Drive," she answered from memory, loving the warmth of the house and knowing Holden and Tim would be happy there.

The woman looked at her computer for a few minutes, then turned in her chair and called out to someone in an office behind her. "Jen, is the Elmwood house sold?"

"Yes, this morning," her sister's voice floated through the office.

It was as if time had gone back, and they were yelling through the house when Mom was away. It was her sister.

"Shoot, it's sold, but we have a ton of nice houses for sale. If I could get your name and number, we could look at something for you." The woman smiled, but Dylan had no interest in anything else.

"That's okay. That was the house I wanted." She hadn't been ready for it to be gone, to have someone else living in their house.

She walked out of the building and let out a long sigh—she had waited too long, and now her dream was gone. Maybe that meant being a part of Holden and Tim's lives was going to be just a dream that she lost as well. So far in life, not much had turned her way. Why would this?

Ten months ago, she had no idea what her life would be like without work. Now, she could do anything as long as Tim and Holden were there. But now their house was gone.

"Jessica?" Jenna yelled from behind her.

Dylan froze mid-step in the parking lot and slowly turned. She looked at her sister, who was no longer sixteen; time had turned her sister into their mother. From the hair to the outfit, she was exactly like Dylan had remembered her mother so many years ago.

"Sorry, not me," she lied. She could never be the Jessica they wanted. For years, she had tried and failed. No longer was she willing to even try.

Turning again, she headed toward her car, it was time to get back to her son.

"Why didn't you ever contact us? Just a letter or a call? Not even once." Jenna started following her. She recognized Dylan. Scar or no scar, her sister knew her.

Dylan let out a huff and wheeled to face her sister, saying, "Because you were better off without me, Jenna. You and mom were a team, you still are. I was never a part of that."

"It was hard to include you when you didn't want to be included," Jenna argued as she looked her over. Dylan knew the moment she saw the scar when her sister's eyes widened in surprise.

"I always wanted to be included, but I didn't want to have to beg. I wanted you two to *want* me there," Dylan hissed.

"She always wanted you there."

"She sent me away."

"She didn't know what to do with you."

"She knew what *he* would do."

Jenn hesitated before answering, "Did he?"

"Every day until I got on that bus to boot camp. She never came back." Dylan said the words, knowing that they had maybe believed that life wasn't so bad for her with Dad. But it had been.

"You never asked her to."

Dylan shook her head and scoffed, "I didn't think I needed to."

"She looked for you! It took her two years to find out you joined the Army, then she started to write to you."

"I know. I have the letters," she admitted, though she knew she shouldn't of.

"Did you read them?"

"Not a one," she said as she opened the back door of the car and grabbed the box with shaky hands. A few letters fell to the floor of the car as she took it out and handed it to her sister. "You can give them back to her. Nothing she can say will be enough to make up for what he did."

Jenna's blue eyes were large as she stared at the box in her hand, taking in the neat rows of letter after unopened letter. "She wrote you all the time."

"When she drove away, it gave Dad permission to do whatever he wanted to me. To do everything he wanted to do to *her*. Do you know what a leather strap does to your back after that many years, Jenna? I do, and so does anyone who sees me naked. No *letter* can heal scars that deep."

Not wanting to see her sister's tears, she turned and got in her car, feeling nothing. No great burden had been lifted, no vindication that she was right, just the continued emptiness she always had, but now she didn't have to carry around that damned box.

Suddenly, she missed the box she had carried around the world with her. Oddly, it had been comforting to know her mother was close, even if just in a letter.

As Dylan drove home, she thought about what had happened, and if maybe she had been wrong to tell Jenna anything. Maybe she had deserved some form of punishment for acting out, but not what her father had doled out every day for months.

Pulling up to the house, she knew it was almost an hour later than she had told Mara she would be. Once Dylan had realized how late she was going to be, she had called Holden's mom to relieve Mara, because she had made an effort last week and Dylan had nobody else to call. Without hesitation, Donna said she would go over and watch the baby for a few minutes.

Jumping from the car, she saw a strange, middle-aged man sitting on the front step. If she was smart, she would turn and leave, but her son was in the house, and she had to make sure he was safe.

Leaving her box behind, she headed right for the man. As she approached, he stood and looked her over.

"Jessica," he said her old name, the one everyone was calling her now.

"It's Dylan," she stated coolly. As she got closer, she realized who it was: Holden's father.

"Sorry, Dylan. Nice day, isn't it?" Glenn Marquez asked. He once accused her of killing his son. Now he wanted to talk about the weather? Yeah, no thanks.

"What are you doing here?" She wasn't in the mood.

"Donna said I couldn't go inside and see the baby until I apologized. So, I'm apologizing," he replied, though he didn't really seem like he liked the idea.

"For what?" There was a lot of bad water between them, and a simple, vague apology wasn't going to cover it.

"For not treating you like the family member you were. Chase married you, and I should have respected that. Instead, I thought I knew better and pushed him away. In turn, pushing you away."

"Every phone call made him think less of himself. I didn't care that you hated me, I cared about how you treated Chase. You where the reason he didn't come home, not me. I hope you treat Holden better."

"The baby's awake," Donna's voice came from inside the house.

Pushing past Glenn, she hurried into the house and grabbed the baby from Donna. The baby was whimpering, and she immediately knew he was hungry.

Taking him back into the living room, she settled him down while unbuttoning her shirt. Oddly, she had been wearing the same outfit most of the six weeks with her son, so changing seemed odd.

When she finally got him settled into feeding, she looked up at Holden's mother. She had moved away from her but was watching.

"Thank you for watching him. Mara had to get to work. I didn't know you would bring Glenn with you."

"He insisted, and he's trying. Not succeeding yet, apparently, but trying. Old habits."

With a knock on the door Glenn, said, "I brought in the box from your car. Some letters were on the floor, and I grabbed them also."

"Put it on the table." She shifted Tim as her father-in-law came in with her box.

He set the box on the table, then shoved the letters into the box, trying to keep them organized.

She watched as he looked into the box, knowing the picture of her and Chase was on the top—the one they took when he was on leave in Florida, two years before he died. They had bought matching shirts and went to the beach, something she really didn't have time for during school but had gone anyway. Sadly, it was the only time she had been to the beach while she was in Florida.

"That was taken during the three weeks Chase was home from Iraq and didn't come home to see you guys. He wanted to spend it with me and knew I was lonely. He should have come here."

"No, no, he probably spent it where he needed to," Glenn admitted, pulling the picture from the box and looking at it closely. Maybe he, too, had a hard time remembering what his son looked like.

She could tell his parents were trying. They were saying the right things, but she had no idea if they truly believed it.

But she knew it was time to leave; time to let Holden start living his life without her. Because the longer she stayed, the more attached she got to everyone around here. Dylan had built a life around no attachments—they just hurt her in the end.

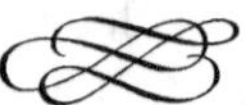

HOLDEN HAD BEEN SURPRISED to see his parents' car at the house when he got home from work. His dad was reading a book to Tim as his mom folded laundry. Dylan herself was reading on her e-reader, but she was still in her fatigues, so maybe she wasn't leaving the couple alone with the baby.

His mom had made his favorite meatloaf, and she told him it was ready soon as he walked through the room to change. His dad barely looked up from his task with his grandson at his arrival. Going into the bedroom, he saw Dylan's box on the floor of the closet, the one that contained everything from her life with Chase. Except now on top were a few letters from her mom, not the picture of her and Chase by the ocean.

Changing into jeans, he wondered what her stuff in the closet meant. Had she completely moved in with him? Had she just missed having the box nearby, so she could look in it periodically and remember how happy she was with his brother?

Dinner went smoothly, though Dylan was silent for most of it. He wondered if his parents had apologized since it seemed like they weren't taking issue with her being there. It was just Dylan who was having issues with them.

Afterwards, Dylan excused herself to go to their bedroom, and he and Tim walked his parents to their car. His mom had nothing but smiles for Tim. And even had a compliment about Dylan and how good of a mother she was.

"You two apologized, right?" he asked, raising an eyebrow at them.

"Yes, but she didn't accept it. She said we would have to earn her trust but could see Tim anyway," his mom said with a half-smile.

"She's not as bad as I always thought," his dad added. "Dylan gave me a picture when I asked about it."

His dad slid the picture of Chase and Dylan on the beach from his pocket. "I'm happy she really loved him." His mom glanced at the picture as well.

"Yes, she did." He wished she could love him as much as she had loved Chase.

"Can we come back again soon?" his dad asked. It wasn't like his dad to want to see his kids and grandkids.

Holden nodded, and Tim nuzzled into his chest. "Sure, just call. Dylan starts work again on Monday," he said and then watched them drive away.

Back in the house, he headed straight for the bedroom to talk to her, wondering why she'd been so quiet.

The door was open, and as Holden walked down the hall, he could see that she had her duffle bag out and was piling her shirts into it.

His step faltered, and he closed his eyes for a moment, controlling his anger. From the doorway, he said, "Tim's hungry."

She didn't look at him as she answered, "There's formula in the cabinet. It's time to start him on that."

"Because you're leaving?" Somehow, he had thought that after getting past the first week deadline, they were going to make it work.

"Yes, you…" She stopped talking as she opened her pants drawer and started picking them up.

"I what? I don't need you anymore? Is that what you were going to say?" he demanded, hating that his voice was raised, knowing she would bolt sooner if he did.

"You and Tim will be better if I'm not here. I should've been gone a long time ago. Your parents reminded me of that." She put the pile in her bag, her emotions fully checked.

"You're his mother, Dylan," he argued.

"Just giving birth to a child doesn't make you a mother. A mother is someone who's there for you always, someone who loves you despite everything...someone you can trust. I am none of those things."

"You don't have to leave, Dylan. Stay at the VA; stay with us." He took a step toward her, his eyes pleading with hers.

"Why, Captain? So I can watch you fall in love and get married and raise my son? All in that gorgeous house?"

"*You* can live with us in that house, Dylan. As a mother to our son and as my wife."

She shook her head. "I don't belong there, and you don't want to settle for someone like me."

"What is so wrong with you, Dylan? Tell me so I understand. How are you so flawed that you can't be a part of your child's life?"

"My father was abusive—to my mother, to me, and to my sister. Mom stayed way longer than she should have but finally got out when I was fourteen. We went with her, only seeing Dad a few times a year on supervised visits."

"Just because your dad was like that doesn't mean you will be. I know you know that."

"Fourteen was too late for me. By that time, I was already abusive to my sister. My mom tried counseling and therapy, but nothing worked. I just got angrier and angrier until I needed to do something."

"How old was your sister?" He sat down next to her, pushing against her so she was leaning against the headboard.

"Two years younger than me," she said, taking the baby from him.

"Tell me about her." He helped her slip off her sweatshirt since her hands were occupied.

"Oh, she was *perfect*," she said sarcastically as the shirt cleared her head.

"Nobody is perfect, Dylan." He fed the words back to her as she adjusted Tim and herself and their son groaned as he started to eat.

"Jenna is and was. Blond hair, blue eyes, cheerleader perfect. She even got breasts before me—I was always a late bloomer. Her prom date was the captain of the football team, and she was just a sophomore."

"Who did you go with?"

"Nobody. I was short, fat, and a nerd. She was friendly and outgoing, and she had so many friends she couldn't step foot outside the house without finding someone to hang out with."

"Someone who wasn't her sister?" He ran a hand over Tim's head as he ate.

Dylan slowly closed her eyes, leaning her head against the headboard. "Yeah, she had no time for me. We didn't have a lot in common."

"Was she scared of you? Did she try to hide from you?"

"No, but she always went running to Mom, telling on me."

"Ah, that was me as well: The Tattler. As the youngest, my job was to tell Mom and Dad *everything* that the other three were doing. It's how I got so good at self-defense: keeping my older brothers from beating on me."

"Did Chase?" she asked, saying his brother's name for the first time. His actual name, not his last name.

Holden chuckled softy. "Before he joined the Army? You bet. Plus, he was in trouble the most, so I had to tell on him a lot." He rolled his eyes, trying to get her to laugh.

"Basic training was hard for him." Dylan gave a half-smile. "Following the rules was a tough concept for him to learn. He knew them, just hated them."

"Why didn't you get married after basic?"

"I didn't want to. We were young and didn't actually know each other well. When we did get married, it was only because Chase was worried. His buddy had been hurt during his last tour, and the guy's girlfriend hadn't been able to go see him. He died a few weeks after getting to Germany, all without her being able to say goodbye. He didn't want that to happen to us."

Holden nodded. He probably would've felt the same way as Chase. "Why did you let my mom take the flag?"

"What flag?" she asked in confusion as she burped the baby over her shoulder.

"The one from Chase's casket. I remember watching her take it from your hands."

"Taking that flag home wouldn't ever be the same as taking my husband home. If she wanted the flag so bad, she could have it. Chase was never coming back."

"But it should have been yours."

"At the time I didn't care, and I really don't care now," Dylan replied with a shrug.

"Where's his ring?"

"I left it on his grave. I was carrying another man's baby, after all, and had to admit our love was over. I had maybe been holding on for too long." Tim, happily fed, burrowed into his mom.

"Did he know about the abuse at home?"

"Yeah. I still had a black eye when we first met."

"Did he at least tell you that you were a kid who made mistakes? That it didn't make you like your father? Because if you were, so was he."

"Not the same. You were just an annoying little kid."

"Dylan, you are *never* going to be a threat to our son. He's never going to know fear at your hand."

She shook her head. "You don't know that."

"Yes, I do, because you loved him enough to let him go. Anyone can love their child, but you loved him enough to make sure he was safe. Even if that meant breaking your heart and giving him to me. I see it every time you pick up another book on raising a baby, every time you check him again to make sure he's breathing, and every time you feed him and kiss his hand."

"But..." she tried to argue.

"No buts—you love him. Being a shitty sister doesn't make you your dad, it just means you were a teenager. We were all shitty people as teenagers, so don't let that be the reason Tim doesn't know you." He took the baby from her arms. Tim had fallen asleep while they'd been talking.

"But what if you're wrong, and I slip up? I don't want to take that chance with our son."

Without a word, he got up taking Tim from her and grabbed her hand, forcing her to follow him. Within minutes they had Tim in his car seat and were driving through town, she was silent as they went. Too silent.

They pulled up to their dream house, and he got out, grabbed the baby's seat, and headed for the door.

"It already sold, Holden. I tried to buy it for you today." She lagged behind him as she spoke, her words holding a pain he hadn't heard from her before.

He stopped and turned to look at her. "You mean for Tim, so you wouldn't have to worry about where he grew up after you left us. Because everything you do is to protect him and make his life better than yours."

Opening the door, he was happy the agent made it there before he did. He needed her to be inside.

"I bought the house, Dylan. For you. Not for Tim, for *you*. So that even if you walked away, you would know where to find us. You'd know where home was." Walking inside, he went toward the kitchen, one of the only places she had been.

"I am not walking away; I have to go. Deep inside, I'm just like my father, and nothing I do can change that." She hung her head but still followed him.

"No, Jessica!" Jan said from the behind them, her voice shaking with regret as she said it, "You will never and have never been Jesse."

Holden stared at his real estate agent, and the truth suddenly slammed into him. Jan Reed and Janet Reed were, of course, the same person. No wonder Dylan had flown off the handle while looking at the house. Her mom had been in it! She hadn't seen the woman in twenty years and hadn't wanted to see her that day, either.

"You don't know me." Dylan spun on her but took a step back as she did.

Janet nodded in earnest. "I once did, and what I knew was that you were kind and sensitive and loving. Those are things your father could never be." Janet tried to close the gap between them, but Dylan kept her distance. She looked like an animal that had been backed into a corner.

"You said I was just like him!" she accused her mother, who flinched at the words.

"No, I never did. I never would."

"You put me in therapy for it. For *years*."

"No, Jess, I put you both in therapy because all you ever saw was abuse. I wanted you to know that wasn't the way life was supposed to be. I wanted you to realize that wasn't how relationships were supposed to be! It was never because of anything you did, it was because of what I did." The pain in her eyes was visible, even from across the room.

"You sent me back to protect Jenna."

"For one moment, I thought she was in danger, yes. When I got home from work that day and found out you had given her a black eye, I lost it. I took you to him, and I never should have. Your sister told me later that she provoked you and that it was her fault you lost your temper." Her mother closed her eyes as a tear fell from her cheek. "She said she did it to see if you would lose it, like a game."

"YOU NEVER CAME BACK FOR ME." Dylan felt her throat start to constrict. *This can't be happening*, she thought.

"You wouldn't talk to me on the phone, and Jesse said you didn't want to come back. He said you were happy and that you were fine."

"I wasn't fine—he beat me every day! Every. Day. I missed school because I was in so much pain I couldn't move. I had cracked ribs when I got to basic training. I had bruises covering my body and a black eye." She pointed to it, though it had healed decades go.

Her mother's eyes went wide. "He said—"

"He *lied*. The scar, the one everyone sees when they see me? The day you dropped me off, he slammed my face into the bathroom mirror, breaking it and cutting my face open. He never took me in for stitches. That was the same day you left me behind."

"But you're not him, Jess."

"I don't ever want to find out. I would rather my son never know me than hate me like I hated him."

"You could never be like him because you know how wrong he was. He never knew it was wrong, Jessica."

"I am not Jessica! Please do not call me that."

"Dylan, then. You are not your father. I should know, I lived with him for far too long."

"You haven't known me for twenty years, and you don't know me now."

"Perhaps, but I see you right now, talking about walking away from the people you love just to keep them safe. But you are not a threat to them. Don't make the biggest mistake of your life, Dylan, don't make my mistake and leave someone you love behind."

Dylan dropped her eyes to the floor, turning away slightly. "I don't even know why you care. I was never perfect enough for you before, but now suddenly, you care?"

"I was just trying to help."

"By telling me I was fat?" she replied, incredulous.

"We had that in common, the two of us could battle our extra pounds together. I always had a harder time connecting with you then Jenna. I didn't mean that I was ashamed of you."

"Yes, you were. Nothing I could do made me as good as Jenna, and she's still right here with you. You don't even care what I do."

"Of course, I do. It's you who doesn't want anyone to know anything about you. If I had my way, I would have both my daughters working for me. Or at least be in their lives."

"There is nothing much in my life. I work."

Janet looked at her flatly. "You have a husband and a son."

"We're not married. Holden is…" She turned and looked at him, who had been frozen for the entire conversation between mother and daughter, just watching. They had never discussed what they were to each other. "I don't even know."

"The man who wants to spend his life with you," Holden jumped in. She had to know how he felt. At this point, he couldn't see his life without her. Tim needed her, and so did he.

"More importantly, he's the man who's taking me home now." She broke eye contact and headed for the door.

Holden hurried after her, worried that she might just take off. He had brought her here to show her the life she so desperately wanted with him and their son, but instead, had he'd accidentally flung her past in her face, a past life she had wanted to forget.

An hour ago, she was almost ready to run, and now she was guaranteed to run. Holden was out of ideas on how to make her stay.

CHAPTER 28

THE RIDE back to the house was awkwardly silent. It had surprised her that he'd been the one that had bought the house. Apparently, they were thinking the same way, just not talking about it.

Seeing Janet at the house had been a shock. After their blow-up, she felt flighty and anguished. She wasn't letting everyone make her think it was all in her head. That she had been wrong the entire time. She knew the truth.

Still silent, they entered the house. Her eyes immediately went to Tim's things: his swing, blanket, and a pile of diapers she had left on the coffee table. Her son was everywhere in their little house.

Back in the bedroom, she grabbed her bag. She needed out of there right now. She couldn't think when Holden and the baby were around.

"You're really leaving?" he asked, taking the baby from the carrier.

"I have to." She tossed the bag by the door and turned to grab her e-reader from the coffee table.

"No, you don't, you're choosing to. Just remember that it is not some altruistic thing you are doing; you're *choosing* to walk away from him." Holden couldn't help the anger from leaking into his reply. How could she still leave?

"There's milk in the freezer, but once it's gone, it's gone. You'll have to start using formula." She ignored his words.

Holden's voice was hollow, numb. "We'll be here when you decide this is all in your head."

"I know me, Captain. She does not, and clearly, you don't either."

"Aren't you even going to tell him goodbye?"

"It's best I don't." She opened the door and grabbed her bag.

"Because even you know you're running away. We love you, Dylan," he said as she shut the door between them, closing off that part of her life.

ONCE AGAIN, Dylan was driving. This time, she had to be back before Monday, which was in three days. No way was she going to her apartment, though—it was too close to Holden and her baby.

Four hours after leaving them, she was in the middle of Iowa and in pain. She wished it was only pain from leaving Holden and Tim, but it was an actual physical pain.

After driving mile after mile away from her baby, the pain was a constant reminder that he needed her. It had been getting steadily worse for the last two hours, and now it was nearly unbearable.

Pulling into a twenty-four-hour super store, she decided there was only one thing she could do to make the pain go away. Once that was gone, she would go on with her life.

An hour later, she was back in the car, short a few hundred dollars, but her breasts were no longer going to explode. The pain was still there, however, just deeper. And there was nothing she could buy to stop that kind of pain.

MONDAY MORNING ROLLED AROUND, and Holden had been sure she would've been back by now. Clearly, he had underestimated Dylan's stubbornness. Now, he wasn't sure he would ever see her again.

Yes, he knew she was starting back at the VA today, but for how long? Would she request a transfer back to the desert? How long would it be before she left?

Today was the first day Tim was going to stay with his parents for the day. No matter how much of a hard time they gave him, they loved Tim and were happy to help out until he found somewhere to put him during the day. He should have been looking even if Dylan had stayed, he knew she wouldn't have given up her job to stay home with their boy.

Tim was happy in his car seat, oblivious to the fact that his mom was AWOL. Well, not oblivious, really. Tim had spent the entire weekend needing to be held, and when Holden held him, Tim either changed his mind or wanted someone else. And his dislike of an actual bottle was the stuff of legends. He had a lot of his mom in him.

With Tim secure and the diaper bag over his shoulder, Holden opened his front door to the morning sun; it was going to be a nice day today. As he stepped onto the porch, he kicked something he couldn't see because of all the stuff he was carrying.

Shifting his load a bit to see what it was, he saw a medium-sized blue cooler sitting there. It looked new and still actually had tags on it.

Holden looked around the neighborhood and wondered who had misplaced their cooler.

Setting Tim's seat and the diaper bag down, Holden crouched to open the cooler. Nestled in the ice were small bags of breast milk. Over a dozen of them, by the looks of it. The cooler was from Dylan.

Holden went back into the house with Tim and the cooler, then set Tim's chair on the table as he unloaded the milk into the freezer. Each was marked with an amount and the date it was filled, all in the sloppy penmanship of a doctor.

He had no idea what it meant, but Holden couldn't help but hope that she wasn't giving up on them completely. Maybe she would still come back to them, once she realized she was wrong.

As long as she was still feeding Tim, there was hope.

CHAPTER 29

"DR. MARQUEZ, your three o'clock failed his pre-op, so there will be no operation today," Jodi, her new nurse, stated as Dylan left her office to head for the operating room.

"How?" she asked in annoyance. She really didn't have time for no-show patients.

"In his words, he 'ate a little bit' this morning, AKA a full breakfast. So, he's been rescheduled, and I guess your day's over." The brunette reminded her a little of Elissa, though some of the bubbliness was missing.

"You can go ahead and head home. I have a few things to catch up on in my office." She turned back to her sanctuary.

"Thanks, Dr. Marquez," Jodi said with a smile and hurried off. Everyone loved leaving early every once in a while.

Well not everyone. Dylan hated it, preferring long shifts That way, she didn't have to think about how empty her life was. Or how easy it would be to fill it.

Her only contact with Holden and Tim was when she dropped off milk every other day. Feeding her son was still her priority, even if she wasn't there.

In the three weeks since she'd left, she had missed them both terribly. Tim was always on her mind—who was watching him while Holden was working? Was he eating? Had Holden transitioned him to formula and no longer needed her milk? Had he forgotten about her already?

She should really stop with the deliveries, but it was her only link, and she desperately needed it. Anything, at this point.

That day, she had also gone cold turkey on Elissa, who in return had stopped talking to her as well. After a few days, she had realized that her "friend" might have been tired of her. Too much calling and needing help, and too little asking about her friend's life. But her friend's life was perfect, so Dylan didn't think there was a need.

Sitting back in her chair, she turned on the computer again to make notes and update charts. It was what most of her day consisted of. No more adrenaline rushes or split-second decisions; everything was mapped out days in advance.

Last week she had started looking for another placement, somewhere more interesting. Every job that seemed exciting had something missing from it: her family. Yes, it seemed Holden and Tim were a part of her now, a part she wasn't ready to leave behind.

Regardless, she didn't know how long she would be able to stay in a job that was not only boring but also within touching distance of a family she couldn't be a part of.

Picking up her phone, she once again flipped through the dozen pictures she had of Tim. Why she hadn't taken more, she didn't know.

She came across one with him in his father's arms, and she started at them both. Holden was smiling, and Tim had his tongue out. It wasn't the best picture ever, but it was the only one she had of them both, and she loved it.

A knock sounded on the door, then flung open before Dylan could respond. "I cannot believe your office looks exactly same as it did in Afghanistan!"

Elissa's voice jolted her, and she nearly dropped her phone. Setting it down, she jumped out of her chair and hugged her friend.

"What are you doing here?" she demanded.

"Long, long story, but the good news is, I requested a transfer here. The bad news is that I'm in the OB."

"Here? Why? I know you weren't happy at work, but your family is there."

"Nope, I took my family with me." She smiled and pulled in a little boy from the hallway, lifting him into her arms. "Ryan, this is Dylan. Dylan, this my son, Ryan."

"Hi, Ryan." She looked at the little boy who resembled his mother with his blond hair and blue eyes. He immediately hid his face in Elissa's shoulder.

"He's tired. It was a long drive," Elissa explained.

"What about Todd? Did he come?" Dylan looked over Elissa's shoulder.

"Nope, he's staying in Chicago."

"Oh, God, Elissa! I am so sorry. What happened? I'm sorry I stopped calling."

"I sort of stopped calling too. He had an affair—well, actually, he had been having an affair for years, but I finally figured it out."

"I am so sorry. Do you have a hotel? If not, you can stay with me," Dylan stated before she could even think about it. Her place was tiny, and Elissa was two people.

"I might take you up on that, because I don't have a ton of money. It costs a lot of money to maintain two families. And apparently, mostly my money."

"Well, it's a good thing I'm done working for the day. Let's go get something to eat before we head home."

"Do you need to call Holden? I can't wait to see Tim."

"Umm, no. We aren't together anymore either. He has the baby… It's better that way."

"What? For how long?"

"Almost three weeks."

"I see," Elissa replied and they headed to the parking lot. After a little discussion of where to eat, they went off in separate directions toward their cars.

At the restaurant, they talked mostly about the past and what they knew about the people they had worked together with over the year they had been in Afghanistan. By dark, Dylan was leading them into the small apartment that had little to no room for guests, even if those guests seemed to have little in the way of stuff.

"Sorry it's small, but I don't usually need much."

Looking at it from the eyes of her friend, she saw it as rundown and sad-looking. It wasn't a home; it was a place she simply occupied for now. At this point in her life, she didn't have one decoration that she took from place to place, just a box.

"We'll sleep in here. It'll be fine, Dylan. Thank you," Elissa said as she ushered her son in. He was more leery of the place than his mom was.

"You two take the bedroom—there's more room, and you've been traveling. I can sleep on the couch." She smiled. They looked ready to drop, and she had gone more than one night without sleep in the past few weeks, what was another?

"If you're sure." Elissa stifled a huge yawn.

"I am. Let me grab clothes for the morning, so you can sleep in." She hurried into the bedroom as Elissa took their suitcase and headed that way also.

After grabbing a few things, she moved the box she had taken back with her from Holden's off the top of the dresser. She had put it down the first day and hadn't moved it since, but now Elissa needed the room, so she would store it in the hall closet.

Elissa gave her a weary smile as they passed and within minutes, Dylan was on the couch, and Elissa and Ryan were in the bedroom, mostly silent. Dylan knew her friend was devastated about her husband, simply because she had never even thought about him straying. Even if there had been offers over the year, she had never even thought about it. Every other word out of her mouth had been about that man and what they'd either done or were going to do. Now he had broken her heart into a million pieces.

She set the box on the coffee table and took out the stack of papers she had received from Holden while they were still in Afghanistan. Looking through the drawings of flowers and trinkets, she suddenly missed getting a new one from him every day.

After folding them back up, she put them into the box and pulled out the letters she had received from Marquez years before. He hadn't been great about writing, but she knew he loved to receive letters from her, so she had sent dozens, while he had only sent a handful back.

After all these years, she didn't need to open them to know what they said—she had them memorized. Either way, it didn't matter what they said… They were from him.

Her maiden name was on them: J. Dylannski. No letters had been received like that after they had married, not that they should have said anything different. When they had married, she had planned to keep her name. Only when she had sent in the paperwork did she change her mind; Chase had never known. It was supposed to have been a surprise when he came back.

Pulling out the pictures of them, she saw a much younger version of herself. They had taken dozens of pictures at the beach that day so long ago, but Dylan only had a few survivors left.

Looking closely at the young man who had stolen her heart so many years before, she could barely remember his blond hair and tried to remember if his eyes were blue or green.

Had she loved him because she needed someone to love, or had their love been deeper than that? When he had died, her entire world had collapsed in a way like never before. He had been her rock, and when he was gone, she had nothing to hold on to. After a while, she didn't hold on to anything anymore, fearing that it would eventually be taken away as well.

She carefully put the pictures and letters back in the box, and as she did, her hand brushed the pile of letters from her mom. Dylan hesitated, but then pulled them out and looked at them as well. "Jessica Dylannski" was written on the top one, though it had been written five years before. At that time, she had been in Afghanistan, but at a different hospital than the last time.

Flipping it over in her hand, she let the other seven or so fall back into the box. The letter was light, lighter than the ones from Marquez.

Carefully and slowly, she opened the letter she had carried from the desert to the States and back again, only to once again be on American soil. Now it was even in the same town it was written in.

It was a one-page letter written on lined paper, and she saw her name at the top. Oddly, when she was little, her mother had called her

Jessie, like her father, but she'd been Jessica or Jess for years before her mom moved them from their house.

How are you doing? I hope you are well. I pray for you every day. They don't say where you are or what you are doing, but you are there and in danger. I worry.

Jenna's daughters made you a care package, but it was returned to us. It seems you never get those—they always come back to us. Jenna has finally agreed to come and work with me. Her job at the insurance agency was cut last summer, and she has been looking for something but hasn't had any luck. Now, she will be working with me! Maybe one day, you can come and work here too. Doug says I'm silly to want to work with my kids, but DJ mostly works with him, so how can I be the silly one?

Happy birthday if these letters are slow. Your birthday card will be in my next letter. I don't know how fast you get these letters, though. I talked to a guy who had been there a few years before, and he said they were slow. He didn't know you, I asked.

I am so proud of you, and no matter what you think, I love you. I made a mistake that I can never change, but I want you back in my life. Even if you can never forgive me for that, I want you to know that I do love you and that I am so proud of who you are and what you're doing out there.

Love always, Mom

Dylan wiped away tears as she opened and read the other seven letters—they were all the same. They all ended the same way, saying she didn't have to be alone and that she had chosen to be alone all along.

Her mother had admitted that leaving her with Jesse Dylannski had been a huge, unforgivable event. Was she willing to admit that she had made just as big of a mistake by never calling her mom. That one call would have gotten her out of that situation, but Dylan had been to stubborn to actually make the call.

Instead, she had taken each and every beating like she deserved it, because in her mind she did. She was just like him. But maybe everyone was right; maybe she was a martyr, punishing herself for the faults of others.

After six weeks with him, she knew there was nothing Tim could ever do that would cause her to abuse him like that. At this point, she was still providing him meals because she couldn't bear the thought that he would go hungry for even a moment.

She had destroyed the only good thing to happen to her in years. She had been callous enough to walk away from her family; not once, but twice in her life. It was beginning to dawn on her that she had made a huge mistake…both times.

CHAPTER 30

TIM WAS EXHAUSTED to the point of crying uncontrollably. Holden couldn't blame him; his life was pretty hard. The little guy spent most of his day entertaining his grandparents, only to be sent home at night with the crabby bear he would one day call dad.

After nearly three weeks, Holden would've thought he'd be used to Dylan being gone, but every day when she wasn't there, he was pissed off again. It wasn't rational, but it was what happened.

So far, he hadn't caught her dropping off the milk. He'd tried, but she was very clever and an early riser. Without fail, there had been a new package for Tim every other day.

Tim had decided bottle feeding was okay, but sometimes when they were alone, he got stubborn and wouldn't drink. Today was one of those days.

Bouncing him as he paced, Holden hoped that the kid would give up and just fall asleep, but so far, that had never happened. At some point, Tim would give in and take the bottle. Holden just had to be patient for a little longer.

After checking the baby's diaper one more time, Holden admitted he was maybe in over his head with his son. He was adorable when he wasn't screaming bloody murder after 10 p.m.

Grabbing the bottle again from the counter, he sat in his recliner and tried to convince Tim to take the bottle, but he wasn't having it. Tim shook his little head back and forth, trying to get the nipple dislodged from his mouth.

The doorbell chimed just as Holden threw the bottle at the wall. Now his neighbors were probably going to complain at him for the noise—he would if it was him on the other side of the door.

Stomping over to it, he swung it open, letting the person on the other side see the sobbing baby in his arms. He was doing his best, so whoever it was could just go and...

It was Dylan, dressed in fatigues, right down to the hat on her head. In her arms was a cooler, one that looked just like a dozen of them that were in his garage.

Her blue eyes were wide with worry and staring at the baby in his arms. Without hesitation, she dropped the cooler and grabbed the baby to her chest.

Relief flooded through Holden, and he picked up the cooler and took it to the kitchen. As usual, he unloaded it in the freezer and set the cooler by the back door.

Returning to the living room, he saw her murmuring something to the baby as she unbuttoned her shirt with one hand. Their son, for his part, had stopped sobbing and was listening to everything she was saying.

Tim's lip quivered as she got the last button undone and arranged her T-shirt and bra until he could get what he had been needing from her. Once he latched on, he actually groaned loud enough for Holden could hear him across the room.

"He wasn't taking a bottle tonight," Holden said softly, not wanting to spook her.

"Does it happen often?" She took Tim's hand and kissed the back of it, just like she always did.

"Every few days," he admitted, nodding.

"Umm, Elissa came to town and is staying with me, but really, I have no room."

He looked around the house. "We have no room either."

"I was thinking that it would just be me. Just for a few days. I don't know her plans yet. She's being transferred here, so she has a job but no place to live. And she brought her son."

"Why the big move?"

"Her husband was cheating, and she needed to get away."

"I see. You can stay until Friday, which is when we're moving into the house. Then you can stay at our home—your home."

"We'll see what happens. He has gotten so big."

"It happens when you miss weeks of his life," he said as she got up to put the baby in his bed. Tim had passed out.

"I know, I needed time." She sighed. Dylan laid him in the middle of the crib and ran her hands over his entire body. He didn't know what she was looking for, but apparently, she needed to do it.

"Did you get enough of us? Or will you be leaving again now?" Holden furrowed his brows in a mixture of frustration and sadness. He needed to know. If this was temporary, he needed to know that now and not get used to her being there.

"I realized that no matter how far or fast I run, my heart will remain here." She turned back toward him, and he led her out of the room.

"Tim will always be home for you. Nothing you do can make him not a part of your life," Holden said, grabbing her around the waist. He pulled her to him, and she went willingly, snaking her arms around him as well.

"Not just Tim. You, Holden. *You* are so deep in my heart, and I can't seem to get you out. Somewhere along the way, you romanced me into loving you." Her voice cracked with emotion, and she buried her face in his chest.

"What about Chase?" Holden's heart skipped a beat. He needed to hear the words, even if she still loved his brother more.

"He will always be my first love, but you are something entirely different. I love *you*, Holden."

Grabbing her ass, he pulled her into his arms as her legs wrapped around his. He had been dying to kiss her since she had first walked back into the house. Breathless, she asked, "Is that good or bad?"

"Good, Dylan. So very good."

CHAPTER 31

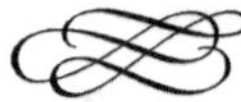

F‌OR THE FIRST time since she started working at the VA, she was nearly late for work. Not only had she slept late and not wanted to get out of bed, but just holding Tim had taken more time than she had allotted.

She called Elissa on her way to work, not even stopping at the apartment as she had planned. Elissa and her son Ryan were going to spend the day at the apartment, maybe head out and get to know the city if they wanted to.

By five p.m., she had sent along an invitation for supper with Holden and Tim to Elissa. From the text she received back, it was making the woman's day to see the baby.

After a long, boring day, she headed out of the hospital. Today she would go home to Holden and Tim. No more hiding from the fact that she belonged there, no more pushing away everyone who happened to get close. She had to accept people into her life; she needed people in her life.

Starting with one person–the one who had missed her when she had convinced herself that nobody had. Maybe if she had read the first letter that came, her life would have been different.

Getting out of the car, she walked into the real estate office for the second time, only this time she hoped her mother would be there. And possibly her sister.

"Can I help you, officer?" the same brunette as before asked.

"Is Janet in?" She pulled off her hat, once again forgetting she wore it. For the first time, wished she wasn't in her fatigues.

"Sorry, she has gone home for the evening. Can I leave her a message?"

"Just tell her I stopped by," she said, regretting not calling.

"Who is 'I'?" The brunette grinned at her question.

"Dylan. Jessica Dylan." She stumbled over her own name. Did her mom even know her as Dylan? Did she remember that was the name she went by now? Should she just say Jessica?

"Jessica Dylan?"

"Dylan Marquez," she answered more comfortably. No matter what happened with her mother, she was no longer Jessica, and would never be again. She had been Dylan for too long now.

"Does she have your number?" the woman asked politely.

Rambling off the number, she gave the woman a small smile and headed for the door.

"Do you have a message for her?" the woman called after her.

"Just tell her I trust her," Dylan said and walked out of the office. The woman had no idea what the message meant and maybe she wouldn't even give it to her boss. It didn't matter; Dylan was willing to trust someone again.

The drive home was short, and by the time she got there, Elissa was hugging on Tim and talking a mile a minute with Holden. Ryan even seemed happy as he ran around the front yard with a toy airplane.

They saw her and immediately headed her way, welcoming her into the group as if she belonged—because she did.

SATURDAY STARTED EARLY, but thankfully, it started with Dylan in his arms. She even complained about him getting out of bed until he returned with Tim for breakfast. To his surprise, she had started feeding the baby anywhere in the house, no longer needing a certain chair for it. Dylan soon became consumed in loving on their son, making Holden chuckle as he got up and headed for the shower.

Once he got out, she had already changed the baby into his moving clothes, which consisted of the tiniest jeans Holden had ever seen, and a white T-shirt, all bought by Elissa the previous day. To his surprise, the two had went shopping after work, leaving him with both boys. It had been an adventure in parenting for him.

By the time they had come home, they had bag after bag of stuff for the new house and Tim. Holden couldn't help but feel that she was getting ready to actually have a home. *About damn time, Dyl.*

Holden grinned at Tim, who was reaching out to him and drooling all over the place. Holden took over the baby so that Dylan could shower, but only after he kissed her and told her he wished they could shower together.

She giggled when his kiss lingered, then let out a full-on laugh as he swatted her on the ass on his way out of the bedroom with Tim.

When Dylan finally emerged in leggings and an Army T-shirt, most of the house was empty. It was odd that the entire house fit in the back of four pickup trucks. In fact, the fourth wasn't even full.

His parents had been the first to volunteer to help with the move. They had also been the ones who said they didn't need to hire anyone to do it.

Next had been Jake and Mara, who had even offered some furniture that they were not using anymore. Which was a good thing because the new house was twice the size of the old house and neither of Holden or Dylan had much.

Roark and Karin had come to help as well. Roark hadn't been impressed with the fact that she'd been Chase's wife. Some old prejudices would linger until he actually met her, but Dylan was able to win people over quickly and wasn't worried.

"Dylan, this is Roark and Karin. They have two girls, Sophie and Katie," he had introduced them.

"We've met," Roark stated coldly.

Dylan tried to hide a smile. "I suppose we did, but we didn't spend enough time getting to know each other." Dylan feigned wistfulness as she filled a box with stuff from the kitchen drawers.

"So, you moved from one brother to another?" Roark commented.

"Yup, all in the short span of fifteen years. Crazy how my evil plan worked out so well." She closed the box and gave her best evil laugh, causing Roark to crack a smile.

"Well, I like someone who's in for the long game," he admitted, taking the box from the counter.

"That's me. Sorry I fell for two of the Marquez brothers. Next time I'll try to find someone else, but there are just so many of you!" She grabbed another box to fill and gave a dramatic shrug, causing Roark to bark out a laugh. Maybe they'd be friends after all.

"You'll have to settle for Lane; I'm happily taken. So, where're all your stuff?" he asked as she filled the new box.

Roark had helped move Holden in and knew what he had, and even he must have noticed that there wasn't much new stuff in the place. There definitely wasn't anything that had a "woman's touch" to it.

"I can fit everything I own in my duffle. It's already packed." She emptied another drawer as she said it.

"Oh, thank God. I did *not* what to spend my entire day doing this." Roark laughed and took the boxes out to the waiting pickup.

Across town, the caravan pulled up to 506 Elmwood Drive, and everyone got out to take a tour of the house before the moving began. Everyone loved the open spaces and the large backyard.

"I don't think we have enough stuff to fill this place." Holden wrapped his arms around Dylan as his brother, father, and Jake argued about the size of a swing set that would fit in the backyard.

"I don't know if we will ever have that much stuff. Maybe we should've gotten something smaller." Dylan settled her arms over his and leaned back into him.

"After everyone leaves, would you rather go furniture shopping or have sex in every room in the house?" he whispered in her ear, loving how her breath hitched at the words.

"Sex, for sure," she chuckled as she turned in his arms. "Furniture can wait."

"Love you, Dylan."

She kissed his neck. "Not as much as I love you, Captain."

Suddenly, he wished that everyone would just leave so that the two of them could start christening the rooms, one at a time. At this point, he didn't even care if they went slow or fast, as long it was with her.

"Alright you two, break it up," Jake said, coming in from the backyard. Mara then came into the room holding Tim, and above them, they could hear the five other kids running around the top floor.

"Never," he growled and swung Dylan into his arms. Her laughter filled the room.

"You're crazy, Captain." Dylan beamed. Today she was using the name not to put distance between them as she always had, but because she loved her nickname for him.

"Only because you're gorgeous, Major." He nuzzled her neck.

"Wait! She outranks you?" his brother asked in amazement.

Holden smiled. "Well, yeah, she's been in longer," he reminded the group. It had never mattered that she had a higher rank than him. She was a doctor, after all.

"Time to get stuff moved in so we can get out of here and leave the two lovebirds alone," Donna said off-handedly, not caring about ranks at all.

"Mom's right." Holden sighed, not wanting to let go of Dylan. Not ever.

"Ladies, let's stay inside while the guys bring in the heavy stuff!" Mara called out above the crowd.

"Agreed," Elissa stated, "bring the table first!"

Mara and Elissa had become fast friends the moment they met, acting as if they'd known each other forever and not just a few days. It was Mara who had suggested that Elissa rent Holden's little house, also offering to help scrounge up furniture for her and Ryan. In fact, when they were done here, they were heading out to get a pickup full of stuff for Elissa's new place.

The guys reluctantly trudged out of the house to carry in all the stuff that Holden and Dylan had accumulated over the last few months. Dylan had so little that she was probably going to bring it in herself.

An hour later, the entire house was a mess of boxes and furniture, but nearly everything was inside. Dylan tossed another empty box in the general direction of the back door. She wasn't used to the clutter and disorganization and needed to clean up ASAP.

A couple of feet away, Mara and Elissa were talking about all the disgusting things little boys do. Dylan was trying not to pay attention but couldn't tune them out either, and every once in a while, they made sure she was listening by teasing her about Tim, saying that he'd do it all too one day.

"Can we talk about something other than bodily functions?" she demanded, causing them both to laugh at her. Dylan just squinted at them.

"Nope, it's the number one topic of discussion at my house," Mara replied.

"Anything else?" Dylan opened another box, which was full of Tim's clothes.

Closing it again, she took it from the kitchen and to the entry where she ran into Glenn, who was holding a large bouquet of flowers.

"Nice flowers, Glenn, are they for Donna?" she asked with a grin. He didn't seem like the flowers type of guy.

"Nope, they're from Holden." He shifted them her way.

Setting the box on the floor, she gladly took them from him. There were so many flowers in it, she couldn't name half of them. She took them into the kitchen and finally got the women to stop talking about their little boys and where they had been caught peeing.

Placing it on the table with a flourish, she took out the card and read it:

I'm never going to stop romancing you--Holden.

"Pretty! What does it say?" Mara asked, looking over her shoulder.

"Nothing you need to see," she replied with a wink. Though the card wasn't anything big, it was huge deal to her. "But I think I'm gonna go look for Holden and say thank you."

As Dylan practically skipped out of the room, Elissa said something that made Mara laugh, and Dylan was sure it was about her. Well, 90% sure.

Upstairs, she looked in their almost-empty room. Their bed was set up, but it had no sheets or blankets on it yet. Next, she went into Tim's room—it, too, was empty of people, but his room was entirely done and ready for him. Donna had taken charge of him today so that she and Holden could concentrate on moving.

A quick check of the other bedrooms had her finding all the kids in one of the closets. They had managed to lock themselves inside and were happy to be free again. Laughing at them as they ran off, she headed down the stairs. The house was getting in shape, though Holden was right—they didn't have enough stuff to make it look lived in. They would make it a home together, though, so she didn't worry.

She eventually found people outside, but still no Holden. Apparently, he had gone to get lunch with his brother, leaving Jake alone to haul stuff in. "They're on 'break,'" Jake told her, adding a sarcastic eye roll for good measure.

Since she couldn't thank him properly yet, she went to her car to get her stuff. It seemed odd that she had insisted on moving her own stuff herself, but it felt right. She needed to be the one carrying her lone bag into her new home, a home with Holden and their son in it.

Shouldering her duffle bag and picking up her box, she headed inside, picking up her latest card from Holden along the way and tucking it into the box. It was another new keepsake for her, and one day, they wouldn't all fit in the box anymore.

She tossed the duffle and box on the bed, then started emptying her duffle into the dresser. She still had only a couple of things to wear but was adding to them as she needed. Yesterday she had worn her Grand Canyon T-shirt, and Holden had teased her about it a little, saying that he didn't recognize her in "civs," which is what they called regular clothing.

"Thanks again for the picture," Glenn said softly. She looked up and saw him leaning in the doorway, watching her.

"What picture?" she asked. She hadn't given him anything today.

"The one of you and Chase. He looked happy in it."

Dylan smiled. "He was, I think."

"Was it taken before or after you got married?" he asked.

"Two years before. We didn't have any pictures taken at the wedding or after it. It was a rush job in the end. Marquez kept insisting, and I finally gave in."

"He *was* persistent. All our boys are, if you hadn't noticed." He chuckled.

"I noticed."

"I was hard on Chase, I know that. Looking back on it now, I see how it destroyed our relationship. I always blamed you for that, but it was me. I pushed the Navy thing on him when he didn't want it. Hell, even Roark hated the Navy. Maybe if he'd gone Army, he would have been happier too."

"Marquez felt like he never met your expectations, even when he did everything you asked of him," she said, saddened a little by the memory. "Maybe if he had gotten older, you could've straightened it out." She placed all her pants in the same drawer she had taken them from yesterday; they still didn't fill it very much.

"I'd like to think so. He was cocky and so confident in himself all the time. I hated that about him. Somehow, I felt I needed him not to be that way. It was dangerous."

"It made him Marquez." The man she had loved had been so sure of himself, and it was what had first drawn her to him. It was also the reason it took so long for her to believe he wanted her, because he could have anyone. "When he died, I felt I failed him."

"You didn't fail him. He died doing what he loved. I, myself, have had to come to grips with that. I took his death hard, harder than I should have, and it took years to come back from it."

"How many?" He looked back up at her, eyes curious.

"Fifteen, but it wasn't until I met Holden that I was able to really let go of Chase. Maybe I needed another Marquez to get me to live again." Dropping the T-shirts in the drawer, she wondered how long she would have lasted if Holden hadn't showed up. What would she have done if she'd been sent home and not been carrying Tim?

"I raised some pretty great boys."

"I know, I can't stop falling for them. Though to tell you the truth, I did fight it pretty hard most of the time."

He laughed and gave a genuine smile, the first she'd seen from him. "You deserve them both. If only I could go back and be a better man when you were with Chase."

"It would be easy if you could, but a life worthwhile is never that easy, is it?"

CHAPTER 32

IT HAD BEEN three days since the big move, and everything finally had a place. Dylan made sure of it. After everyone left that Saturday, she had spent the next several hours putting things away and then moving everything around again until they were perfect.

That Sunday, they had finally spent the day in their house with their son. It had been perfect. For lunch, Holden had even taken her on a picnic in the backyard. Since Tim was napping, it had been just the two of them. He had insisted on her wearing her T-shirt from Pike's Place Market, not that she didn't look sexy in her Army one, but this was something different.

They sat on the blanket together and talked, and she finally opened up about the abuse she had endured when she was eighteen and why she'd been so upset with her mother. It had been unbearable, but she had also been too stubborn to call her mom. At the time, joining the Army had seemed like the only option to Dylan, but it had been the Army that had steered her toward medicine and made her who she was.

She had even told him about the letters, most of which were back with her family. But the ones she'd kept had made her realize that her life could have been different if she had reached out to them. Her mom had loved her and wanted her back, all while Dylan stubbornly thought she had nobody.

It was those letters that sent her back to them, because ultimately, Dylan was the reason her life had seemed so lonely. She wanted to change that, so she did.

Her mom hadn't reached out to her yet, which saddened her because she thought her mom wanted a relationship with her. But she had gone this long without her mom and now had a family of her own. She needed to focus on them.

Now she was more relaxed now than she had ever been during the six weeks she had spent raising Tim with Holden. No longer was she reading books on raising a baby; she was just being a mom, realizing that mistakes would be made and could be corrected.

She was laughing more and was almost a different person than the one Holden had met the day Jackson was hurt. The edge and hardness were dulled, and she wasn't working herself to the point of collapse. In fact, she was looking at cutting back a little, mostly because she found stateside surgery boring.

Monday afternoon he walked into the house at the end of the day and found his mom was recapping Tim's day to Dylan as she snuggled the baby close to her. It never got old seeing Dylan loving on their son. She still treated him like a gift she had never thought she wanted or deserved.

"He was just a happy baby today," his mom concluded. Since day one of him needing daycare, Donna had volunteered to fill the roll, loving the opportunity to spend time with the baby. After a few days, she had decided to babysit Tim at their house instead of him bringing the baby to her. All his stuff was at home, and she didn't have to keep a lot of it at her house.

"He always is, aren't you, Tim?" Dylan asked the baby as she kissed his little fingers.

"He is. Well, I better get home before Glenn thinks I've run off." Donna chuckled.

"Oh, he'll go looking for you, I'm sure."

"Maybe once, but not anymore."

"Once and still, Donna. I'll tell Holden to give him some pointers on being romantic."

"I'll get right on it," Holden said as he came in from the entry; he hadn't meant to eavesdrop.

"No need, your dad isn't one for that."

"I'll do it anyway." Holden hugged her and followed her to the door. He was serious about talking to his dad—his mom deserved to know she was loved also.

"See you tomorrow," his mom said as she headed out the door. It was working out great to have her there.

After closing the door behind her, he headed to find the love of his life and their son. Now that the kitchen was empty, Dylan had vanished from that half of the house, and Holden found her in the living room getting ready to feed the baby. Though he wasn't crying, he was happy lunch was being served.

"How was your day?" she asked as she shed her button-up shirt and laid it on the arm of a chair.

"Good, and yours?" His eyes were on her bare breasts the moment before his son latched on. This was still his favorite thing to watch.

"Okay, but I got a call from the ER today about an opening. It seems they want to open more of a trauma center and need surgeons on staff. It would be way closer to what I was doing in Afghanistan."

"Sounds interesting." He didn't know if he liked her going to back to the exhausting work she was doing, though.

"I think so too. They're trying to get three surgeons. I would have to work a forty-eight-hour shifts every week, but then I'd get the rest of the week off. I would have to put in another twenty-four-hour rotation every third week, but most weeks I would have five days off to spend with Tim."

"Did you say yes?" he asked as he leaned against the doorframe. They had never talked about work schedules before, but it seemed so…normal.

"Not yet. I wanted to hear what you thought about it."

"You want it?"

Dylan stole a quick peek at him, then looked back at Tim. "Yes."

"Why?"

"Because I can spend more time with Tim, and I hate the routine of my current job at the VA. I like the excitement of the desert, but I can't leave you guys."

"You don't think you'll get bored with all that time off?"

"Not with Tim, no. And I want Elissa to work with me. They said I could bring along my nurse. We can pal around together on those days, and Ryan too, of course."

"And she says…?" he asked, knowing she would have talked to her already.

"She likes the idea, and I'm thinking that either Mara and Jake or your parents would help with Ryan. And you, sometimes. We have to be her family; she has nobody here," she reminded him, not for the first time. It seemed she was way more concerned about her friend than she had ever been about herself while in the same situation.

Holden couldn't help but smile at his amazing, gorgeous wife who cared for so many people. "We will. If that's what you want, we can make it work. I can attest that you're a great emergency surgeon. When would you start?"

Dylan beamed. "Next week. The two other doctors are as ready as I am."

"Good thing we already have all those coolers for the milk you'll be bringing home with you," he teased.

When she had admitted she couldn't stop providing milk for Tim while they were separated, he knew she had started losing the battle of independence. Tim was a part of her and would be forever.

"You're being mean, Captain. And after I got you a present," she said petulantly. The baby was no longer suckling but sound asleep in her arms, just where he liked to be.

"I got you a present also. You first." Holden sat down next to her on the couch.

With a flourish, she pointed at the wall above the fireplace. They had no pictures when they had moved in, so the walls were still mostly empty. But now, leaning against the fireplace was a framed picture of black and white flowers.

"Is that one I gave you?" He got up and looked closer at it, remembering how he had given it to her so long ago.

"The first one. I had it framed to remind us of how far we've come." She didn't move, just sat with Tim.

Turning to her, he grinned. She just admitted she loved the romance. Not in so many words, but still.

"All this time you scoffed at my romantic ways, and now here you are being the romantic one."

"I never said I didn't enjoy it, just that you needed do it. I kind of liked you from the start."

"And I liked you way more than I should have. *Way* more. My brother had great taste in women."

"I wonder what Marquez would think of us?" she asked, looking out the window, probably at the sky.

"He'd think I'm the luckiest guy around. He may have been your first love, but I'm going to be your last." His heart started pounding as he crossed the room and got down on his knee in front her. She didn't notice because her eyes were still on the window.

"I hope so," she said dreamily. Holden could see the faint, wistful smile pulling at her lips.

"Dylan, will you marry me?" he asked, because she was lost in her own thoughts and he wanted her forever.

"What?" She turned and looked at him, eyes widening as her mind raced to catch up.

"Marry me. You don't even have to take my name," he joked.

"You bought a ring?" She looked as if she was trying to decide if she was simply imagining things.

"Well, that's what you do when you ask someone to marry you," he hesitated, wondering if she was going to say yes.

"It's *beautiful*."

"Are you saying no?"

"No."

"Oh, okay. This just became awkward then."

"What? I mean no, I am not saying 'no.' I'm just surprised, is all."

"Does no-no, mean yes?" Now Holden was totally confused. And his knee was starting to hurt.

Dylan let out a joyful laugh and said, "Yes! Yes, I would love to marry you."

~

MONDAY CAME QUICKLY, and suddenly, she was leaving her baby for two days straight. Dylan worried that she hadn't thought this through enough and that maybe she should just go back to boring surgeries at the VA and leave the "leaving babies alone for days on end" to someone else.

"Dylan, I'm here," Donna's voice rang up the stairs. Her shift started at nine, so she still had a little time, but Donna must have realized she'd be a little frazzled this morning.

Frazzled? I never get frazzled, Dylan thought. Today was the first time in years she was anything close to frazzled. The doorbell rang as she got Tim dressed in his moose pajamas. Elissa would be there to drop off Ryan, and they would drive together to work. It was her first day on this shift also, and she was leaving her kid with virtual strangers, so others had it worse than Dylan did.

Dylan headed down the stairs in black slacks and a light blue blouse. She felt a little weird in her new outfit; she wasn't used to wearing something other than fatigues to work. Even in the surgical department, she usually wore them.

Now she was required not to look like a soldier since her roll in the emergency room, she' would be seen by the civilian public. Therefore, no fatigues.

"Okay, Tim is fed and changed and changed again. Blow out. But he should be good for a few hours." She headed down the stairs with Tim in her arms. Though he was sleeping, she didn't want to miss a moment of time with him. She would be gone for two days and needed to soak up every last second.

"Got it. I answered the door when you were upstairs," Donna said a little sheepishly, as if she wasn't allowed to.

"Was it Elissa?" she asked, not hearing Ryan, which she usually could if he was within a mile.

"No, it was me," Janet Reed stated from behind her future mother-in-law.

"Oh, I didn't think I would see you." Dylan reflexively pulled the baby closer.

"Amanda misplaced your slip, but I found it this morning. I didn't think you would be home, but I had to try. I couldn't wait to see you again." Her mother looked at her from top to bottom, and Dylan started wondering what she thought of the semi-professional look she was trying to pull off.

"Usually, I'm not, but this is my first shift in the ER," she replied causally. Holden's mother had moved towards the kitchen, giving them some privacy.

"I'm really sorry for everything I did back then, Dylan. I never realized that you thought I didn't love you. I never preferred your sister over you. I loved you both equally," Janet insisted.

"It didn't feel that way."

Janet nodded. "And that's all my fault. Same with believing Jesse that you were happy and healthy with him. I should've known better. I believed his lies again. I should have known better."

"I should have called, but somehow, I had convinced myself that I couldn't. My only escape was the Army, so I took it and didn't look back. Until Holden."

"He's a very nice man, and you're very lucky to have found him." Her mother smiled.

"He deserves all the credit; I wasn't that easy to get close to, but I'm so glad he kept chipping away."

"How about I take him from you so you can get to work?" Donna came back from the kitchen and reached for Tim. Dylan let him go willingly.

"Oh, Donna, I'm sorry! Janet Reed is my mother. Janet, this is Donna Marquez, my mother-in-law." It still felt odd to say that, and glancing at her ring, she realized she should have said *future* mother-in-law. The two women didn't shake hands but looked at the baby instead, as if in agreement that he was the most important thing.

"I thought you weren't married to Holden yet?"

"When I was 22, I married his brother, Chase. He died a few weeks later. Holden and I ran into each other last year in Afghanistan. We clicked, I guess."

"You were over there all the time. When I would talk to other families who had kids or husbands over there, their tours were always less than a year, but you were there for years on end. I was so scared for you."

"I was never in danger; I never left the base. Medical personnel doesn't unless they're field medics, and I was never that."

"You became a nurse? You always talked about it. I was skeptical, but every few months, you'd bring it up," Janet said with a smile. "I am so happy you fulfilled that dream. I wish I had believed in you more."

"I tested well in medicine and knew that when I left for basic, I would be heading to college, not war when it was over. I lucked out. Chase and I met at basic, but he went to war."

"Are you staying here?"

"Yes, I have twenty years in now, so I can say where I want to go at this point. If they want to send me back to Afghanistan, I can get out."

"Would it be possible for us to have lunch sometime? I don't want to lose you again."

"I would like that. It might take a little to get over everything, but I'm willing to work on it if you are—" Her words were cut off as Janet hugged her tight, tighter than she remembered her ever hugging her before. Not that she remembered many hugs while she was in high school.

"I love you, Jess…Dylan. *So* much."

"Love you too, Mom."

Within moments, the front door flew open, and Ryan ran into the room with all the energy of a five-year-old. His mother walked in after him more sedately.

"I cannot believe you talked me into more twenty-four-hour shifts. Hell, this one is forty-eight hours!" the blond said. She was dressed in dark red scrubs; no need for semi-formal for her. *Lucky.*

Dylan's mom let her go at the sudden intrusion of more people. Turning slightly, she looked at Elissa and Ryan.

Dylan grinned at her friend and replied, "But then you get five days off, not two."

Elissa tossed a bag of her son's stuff on the floor and groaned, "Only you could talk me into something like this."

"I know, don't you love me?"

Elissa rolled her eyes. "I must, because I'm working with you again."

"I missed my favorite nurse."

"Are you going to be as demanding as you were overseas? Or have you relaxed at little?"

"Oh, not in the OR. Elissa, this is my mother, Janet Reed. Mom, this is my nurse, Elissa."

"Oh, my God! You have a *mother*? What happened to you being hatched? I'm still going with hatched." Elissa laughed at her own joke. "Just kidding, your daughter is an amazing surgeon, Ms. Reed. I have worked with a number of them over the years, but Dylan has great hands."

"Surgeon?" Her mother turned and looked at her, clearly surprised.

"I tested very well," Dylan replied, nonchalant.

"I didn't think you would make a good nurse, and I never thought you would go beyond that."

"The Army thought I could, so I did."

"Dylan, if you and Elissa don't leave now, you'll be late," Donna said after glancing back at the clock on the microwave.

"Yeah, we have to get to work." Dylan was glad the woman had been keeping an eye on the clock; they couldn't be late the first day.

Elissa gave Ryan one last hug before heading out the door, and Dylan kissed her baby and followed her. Oddly, leaving the two women in charge of her son—two women she hadn't trusted or liked a year before—didn't worry Dylan at all.

CHAPTER 33

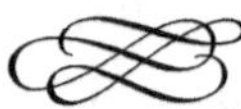

WEDNESDAY DRAGGED BY FOR HOLDEN, who now understood why Jake hated working when Mara was off. He hated being at the office when she was home. Even worse, she was home in bed without him.

"Did she at least call you and tell you how it went?" Jake asked. The office had been dead all day.

"Yes, at lunch. She played with the baby and was crashing. My mom was taking him home with her, so I have to pick him up."

"Right after work?" Jake grinned.

"Nope, she can keep him for a bit longer." His parents were completely on Dylan's side now. She had wormed her way into their hearts without even trying. Some of it had to do with Tim, but a lot of it had to do with how much she had actually loved Chase, and now him.

"How was her shift?"

"Good. A few surgeries, but there was some downtime in between. Enough time to talk to her mom again, so we're having supper with them later in the week—her mom and stepdad and her sister and her husband. It's going to be hard, mostly because I haven't forgiven her as easily as Dylan has."

"She's changed a lot, even from before when she was taking care of the baby."

Holden shrugged. "She just let her guard down and decided not to let other's opinions of her matter anymore."

"Why don't you head out a little early and surprise her?"

"If you're sure, I would love to," he stated, already getting up to leave.

"Yup, but you owe me." Jake chuckled as Holden practically ran out of the building.

Twenty minutes later, he was home and had his boots off and was stripping as he climbed the stairs to their bedroom. By the time he found her sleeping in bed, he was down to his boxers and slid into bed beside her.

Without waking, she nuzzled closer to him. To his delight, she was naked under the covers. Holden closed his eyes and said a silent prayer of thanks. He *loved* finding her naked. He loved being around her all the time, but naked and baby-less was going to be *great*.

"You're home early," her voice was groggy as she burrowed even closer to him.

"Jake let me go, so I could spend time with my fiancée." He ran a hand up her body.

"He's a nice guy," she purred, rolling over to face him. Her blue eyes were brighter than normal, sparkling with mischief.

"How was your day?"

"I spent time with Tim and slept, so it was pretty easy. Donna was nice enough to take him to her house, so I could get some sleep. Did you stop and get him?" she asked, hands warm and adventurous as they skimmed over his chest.

"No, I was going to pick him up later."

She winked at him. "Good. I need a little time with my captain."

"Holden," he answered automatically.

"Him, too, but they're so much alike, I can't tell them apart sometimes."

"You're wearing my ring." His finger followed the chain from her neck to her breast.

"I can't wear it when I work. I forgot to move it to my finger." She looked down at it.

"Did you wear Chase's ring like that?"

Chuckling, she said, "No, it never actually fit. I never got around to resizing it, and then he was gone. At that point, I had started med school and couldn't wear it much anyway." As she talked, he unclasped the necklace and slid it from her body.

Slipping the ring off, he put the necklace on the nightstand and slid the ring back onto her finger. "I like it better here, though I like that it's my ring by your heart as you work now."

"I don't need your ring there, Holden, you're always there."

He looked at her intently and asked, "Are you still thinking about leaving? Do you still think you are a danger to Tim?"

She thought about it for a moment before answering. "Sometimes the feeling is overwhelming, like I can't even breathe because that would hurt him. But I can't leave him again. He's a part of me now, and nothing I do will ever change that."

"You're ready to stay with us forever?"

Dylan moved to climb on top of him and straddle his hips. She placed a kiss on Holden's neck, just below his ear. "If I could have left you, I would have. Believe me, I tried."

Holden closed his eyes, feeling the warmth of her on top of him. He wrapped his arms around her, pulling her even closer so that her chest was pressed against his. "I'm glad you couldn't do it."

"Me too, Captain, me too."

EPILOGUE

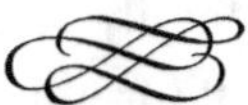

It was always hard the first day after a forty-eight-hour shift. After sleeping most of the day before and barely sleeping the night after, Dylan always found herself waking up late the following morning. Today she was grateful that Holden was home for the day to take over parenting duties.

Over the last three years, he had never complained about her long hours, probably because she tried to make up for it on her days off. It was those days she cherished most of all. It seemed that even though she was working full-time, she wasn't missing a lot of her son's growing up. Even now, she couldn't see herself going back to regular hours anytime soon.

Elissa even enjoyed it, and they usually spent a good amount of their off time together, and with Mara when she wasn't working. The two had turned into Dylan's best friends and had bonded quickly over their sons. Last summer, when Mara had finally had her baby girl, Elissa had been right there in the delivery room. To the hospital staff's dismay, Elissa had also been telling everyone how to do their job.

Dylan quietly walked down the stairs, listening to Holden talk to Tim. The sound of his rich baritone hadn't stopped making her stomach dip, even after all these years. Some days she still couldn't believe that he was really hers. They had gotten married within months of their engagement, and this time, both their families had been present and happy for them.

"Mommy's up!" Holden said, spying her as she came into the room.

Tim was sitting in his highchair at the island, his blue pajamas covered in sticky syrup as Holden made more pancakes on the stove. It was the picture of a perfect family, and it was hers. She promised herself that she'd never take that for granted again.

"Morning, Tim!" She walked by him and kissed his sticky brown curls. At three years old, he looked more like her than his father, but that was something she wouldn't have known if her mom hadn't brought over her baby pictures not long after she came back into Dylan's life.

Holden, still in black pajama pants and Army T-shirt, grabbed her around the waist and pulled her tight to him. Swooping down, he nuzzled her neck while making loud "dinosaur" noises, making Tim scream with laughter. Their son was into all things dino lately, and they were all over the house. Pulling back slightly, he whispered, "Love you, Dylan."

She snaked her arms around his neck and kissed his chin. "Love you too, Captain."

"He's Holden, Mommy," Tim corrected her from around a mouthful of pancakes.

"I stand corrected. Holden, then." She laughed at her kid; he didn't miss a thing.

"Did you sleep well?" Her "captain" didn't let her go.

"The usual." She grabbed a pancake from his stack and took a small bite.

"Is that good or bad?" He always asked.

"I couldn't sleep for a little bit in the middle of the night, but that turned out okay." She ripped off another piece and offered it to him. Holden's face lit up with understanding.

"Just okay?" He pulled her tighter to him, so she could feel that he also remembered how she'd woke him up that night.

"It was pretty acceptable." She laughed at his comically pained expression.

"Unacceptable. We'll just have to try harder next time." He nuzzled her neck again.

"Any harder and it'll kill me, I am over forty now, you know," she admitted as his hand went up her shirt and cupped her breast. His groan at finding it bare was worth leaving her bra off this morning, and Dylan smiled to herself.

A cry from across the room had them both groaning for a different reason. Pulling apart, Holden hurriedly pushed the pan that he was making pancakes in off the burner, the last one was half-raw and half-burned. "I'll take Tim and clean him up; you feed Tuff."

Turning to the playpen that seemed to have become a permanent fixture in the corner of the kitchen, Dylan saw their second son standing up and looking at her over the side. His cries stopped the instant she looked at him. At almost a year old, Tuff was starting to come into his name, one that Holden had insisted on for their second.

He was the spitting image of his dad and as rough-and-tumble as a Marquez boy got. Though under it all, he was a mama's boy through and through.

Picking him up, he held her tight—he always did. Dylan walked with him into the living room and sat in Holden's old ugly chair. She'd never admit it to him, but she secretly it loved as a comfy feeding spot for her boys. From it, she could look at the drawing Holden had made her so long before.

They hadn't really planned on having another baby, but things happened, and it was a more relaxing pregnancy and delivery the second time around.

When Tuff had drifted off to sleep, but she was still holding him when Holden came into the room, now in jeans and a red T-shirt and carrying a clean and dressed Tim. He saw her looking at the picture.

"I should really work on keeping the romance alive." He set the boy on his feet, who made a beeline to the back of the room where his toys were all put away.

"No need; you have me."

"Said no woman ever," Holden replied, smiling. He took the baby from her and walked him into the kitchen, back to the playpen.

Getting up, she followed him and enjoyed the view of his tight, jean-clad ass as he laid their son in the playpen. It never got old. "There's no place I would rather be then here."

"Afghanistan?" he asked, his eyes now on her.

She still missed the rush of being in a warzone, and probably always would. But her life was so much better now than it ever had been there.

"Not really anymore. But this place is going to get a little more interesting in a few months." She strolled up to him.

His eyebrows raised in question, then he grinned at her. Grabbing her, he lifted her into the air and spun her around. She giggled and wrapped her legs around his waist, planting kisses all over his grin.

Pulling back, he demanded, "You're sure?"

"I work at a hospital, so I think I can get a pregnancy test at any moment. It's one of the perks, you know." She ran her fingers through his hair. She absolutely loved touching this man.

"Are you sure you want another one?"

"As many as we can have, Captain. We're pretty good at this parenting thing."

"Can I say, 'I told you so?'" he laughed and squeezed her butt. "I told you s—" He didn't get to finish teasing her, as Dylan's lips claimed his, effectively shutting him up. But he was right and had been the entire time—about everything.

Because of him, her life was perfect, so very perfect. All because he never gave up on her. He romanced his way into her heart, and she had no defense for him. She hadn't stood a chance, and she couldn't have been happier about it.

BONUS EPILOGUE

"I'm not taking three kids anywhere alone again!" Dylan stated as she stumbled into the house after lunch with her mom, carrying two boys through the door. Exhaustion radiated from her. Even her yellow t-shirt was now full of different-colored splotches and had more wrinkles in it than it had when she had left the house. Luckily, her capris were black and hid every stain they'd ever received—Holden was sure there were a few.

Holden had told Dylan before she left that she was going to have trouble with a toddler and a baby who had missed a nap, but he definitely wasn't bringing that up. Not that he was an expert on their children, but he *was* kind of used to them. Even he sometimes had difficulties with Tim and Tuff alone.

"You only brought two." After taking Tuff from her arms, he was met with a scowl.

She gently set their oldest on his feet, who then began to run into the house and away from his parents. "He who has never carried a child should not say I didn't bring this one," she said, pointing at the stomach that still contained baby number three.

"I just meant that he shouldn't have been much trouble, not like these two." He kissed her forehead softly and ran a hand gently over their third child, then cupped her breast because he could. That earned him another scowl.

"Don't say 'he.' We don't know that. I'm rooting for a girl." She let the diaper bag fall to the floor with a thump.

"Only one week until we know." Both were actually dying to learn what gender the third baby was, but Dylan loved the surprise at delivery, and she usually got her way, hence the third baby. Holden had been happy with just two, but Dylan wanted more. No matter how much she liked to complain about the kids, she loved them.

"Don't remind me. This is going to be the longest week. I don't even get to work." With a planned C-section the following week, her surgical rotation had been cut back. Dylan was convinced it was because the other doctors didn't think she could reach a patient past her stomach anymore. But then again, his wife often complained during her final trimester, and a bit in the first two also.

"I know, Elissa has been whining for weeks about having to work with Dr. Narcissist while you're on maturity leave," he joked, hoping to improve her mood. Both women felt the same way about the man.

"Dr. *Narson*. They don't exactly get along." Dylan didn't laugh. In fact, she winced at his attempt at a joke.

"Does Elissa have a little crush?" He set Tuff down to play with his brother, who was taking every toy they owned out of the toy box in the corner of the room. As he always did.

"I hope not. The man is sixty and thinks most women, if not all, should be home raising children. Work is for single ladies." She pushed past him and slumped onto the couch, kicking off her shoes as she sighed.

"Elissa's a single lady." Sitting next to her, he grabbed her feet and pulled them onto his lap. They were swollen, and he knew they were bothering her today.

"Quit trying to set her up with everyone. She isn't ready." Dylan leaned back into the couch to get more comfortable. Not once in four years had she ever suggested that her friend start dating or getting over her failed relationship. Holden wondered if it was because Dylan had taken fifteen years to get over her first love, meaning that Elissa got as much time as she needed from her friend.

"It's been almost four years. As far as I can tell, the man isn't worth that much time. Not to mention, she's cute and shouldn't be wasting her time on that guy. He dumped her; he doesn't deserve her," he argued. After all the years they had known her, she was like a sister to Dylan.

It shouldn't still surprise him how close they were—they had been through a lot together over the years. Elissa's family had mostly been non-existent in her life since she moved here, so Dylan's entire family happily filled that role for Elissa and her son.

Dylan raised a questioning eyebrow. "You think she's cute?"

"Of course, but then again, you're absolutely gorgeous, so there's no competition," he assured her as he continued to rub her feet.

She rubbed her stomach and grimaced. "I look like a beached whale."

"*My* beached whale, and that's the most important part. Such an adorable beached whale." He lifted a foot and kissed her big toe, making her almost smile…almost.

"Shut up."

"I don't tell you enough, but I love you, Dylan.

"I love you too, Captain, but then again, you don't look like a beached whale. Why are you still as hot as the day we met?" She leaned back and shut her eyes, still rubbing her stomach.

"I thought you didn't think I was hot when we first met?" he couldn't help but ask.

"Did you see yourself back then? How could I not think you were hot? Hot and annoying." At least she smiled as she said it.

"I will take the hot part, but in no way was I annoying. Maybe annoyingly handsome and lovable."

This time he got not only a smile but also a small giggle. Then a grimace.

He stopped rubbing Dylan's feet and looked at her in concern. "Are you sure you're okay?"

"Just a twinge in my back. Controlling your kids is harder than it looks." She was still rubbing her stomach, but now with both hands.

"Maybe you should call Dr. Keller."

"No need."

"Why not?"

"Because, you do know that I am a doctor, right? Why would I call another doctor for advice about me?" Her eyes were now open and looking at him, waiting for him to question her abilities. It was obvious that she was preparing for an argument.

"Call Elissa then," he suggested. Even though Dylan was a doctor and Elissa was a nurse, Elissa had years of experience in the OB.

"Even worse! You know how she likes to hold it over my head that she knows more about kids then I do. No way am I calling her!" She grimaced again and adjusted her body on the couch.

"Fine then, I will." He dropped her feet and got up, pulling his phone out of his pocket as he did. Dylan scowled at him as he dialed the numbers.

"Give me that. I'll talk to her." She only held out her hand as her other rubbed her stomach.

The phone rang twice before Elissa answered gruffly, "What can I do for you, Holden?"

"Dylan doesn't want me to call you."

"So, she admits I'm right and that I've always been right?" Elissa laughed at her own answer to an argument that they must've been in the middle of.

"I would love to say yes, but she'd kill me." Dylan's eyes said as much from the couch. "But instead, I'm calling because her back has been bothering her all day, and she doesn't think it's anything to worry about."

"All day like since this morning or all day since she sat down?" It seemed Elissa knew his wife better than him in some ways.

"All day. She went with her mother to lunch and has been uncomfortable and crabby since before that."

"I'll meet you at the hospital. She should be checked out." Her answer was not as comforting as Holden had wanted. He'd wanted her to say that there was nothing to worry about; that everything was great. His wife was just crabby.

"What did she say?"

"That you need to get checked out."

Dylan rolled her eyes. "She doesn't know."

"Call your mom, and I'll call mine," he said. If they were going to the hospital, they needed both parents to know what was happening.

"You call my mom. I just spent hours talking to her." Dylan waved her hand in the air as if they didn't get along still.

"Was your sister there?" he asked as he dialed his parents.

"Yes, of course. Okay, it wasn't bad, just that her life is still pretty perfect." Tuff had walked up to the side of the couch, and she pulled him onto her lap, or chest since there really was no lap. After kissing him, she looked him over, checking this and that, just enjoying their son.

"Isn't *your* life perfect?" Smiling at the scene, he still loved her ability to love their kids without the fear she once had. He was sure she hadn't thought about that around Tim in months, if not years.

"Of course it is, but I don't shove it in her face all the time." Not that she and Jenna weren't close; they were. They just spent too much time competing for their mother's love.

"I can see you being humble like that." He teased Dylan as his mom answered the phone on the other end.

An hour later, the house was completely full of people, and Dylan wouldn't stop talking to any of them.

Everyone in the family had been in attendance at the 'when the baby comes' meeting last month, and they had all been there for the entire process when Tuff was born. But that didn't stop Dylan from going over every point again.

"They know, Dylan." He grabbed her hand and tried pulling her to the car. He had already loaded up their bags before anyone had arrived—he was ready to leave.

"Tim says he doesn't need a nap, but he does," she told his mom, Donna, who babysat for them often.

"I know, Dylan," Donna answered as she shifted Tuff in her arms. All he wanted was to be held by his mom. Tim was in Janet's arms as well, only because he too wanted to be held by Dylan. Janet had picked him up before Dylan could.

"Dylan, we have to go," Holden warned her again.

"One second." She even held up a finger as she said it.

Rolling his eyes, he grabbed her into his arms and carried her from the house. All her anger was immediately directed at him, even if she knew he was right. They didn't have time to go over the entire three-hour meeting from last month if Elissa thought that she was in labor.

"You don't want to have an emergency C-section like with Tim, do you?" he asked her as they made it out into the crisp fall afternoon.

"No," she admitted reluctantly and stopped fighting.

Putting her down so she could get into the car, he stopped for one moment and kissed her lips, still loving the intense feeling it brought. It never got old to kiss this woman.

Rushing around the car, he slid in beside her and took her hand. He knew she would never admit she was scared about the delivery. The last one had been good, but Tim's always made her leery. Though it had turned out great, it was still not something she wanted to repeat.

"Still thinking about naming him Tyler?" he asked. Fighting about baby names usually took her mind off her anxiety.

"Never Tyler—it's Hank." She squeezed his hand.

"I thought we decided to stay with Ts?

"You decided. I didn't agree to anything. Hank."

"I don't think so."

"You named the last one!"

"And you named the first one. What if it's a girl?"

"Dr. Kellen thinks it's another boy."

Holden shrugged. "She could be wrong."

"Nope, it's another boy. Three boys."

"Trip."

"Douglas," she countered as he pulled up to the door of the hospital a few minutes later.

"No way." He pulled her in for one last kiss before she climbed out of the car and headed into the building. It was the same one that their other two children had been born in.

He knew the fighting was for nothing; they would look at that tiny baby and know what to name him. It would be simple once they saw the baby.

～

Five hours later, Dylan opened her eyes and looked around the room. Though they hadn't knocked her out for the C-section, the drugs that they gave her always made her sleep anyway, which she had learned the hard way when Tuff was born. She'd missed the entire birth and even the first few hours of his life.

"You're awake." Holden was holding her hand as he sat in a chair right next to the bed.

"I am," she barely got out. Her mouth was so dry.

Holden helped her drink some water and adjusted the bed so that she wasn't flat on her back anymore. It reminded Dylan of when Tim was born; his patience always amazed her, and always made her love him just a little bit more.

"Everything went great without you," he grinned at her. "The baby was born a little over two hours ago, and the family hasn't come yet. I wanted you to wake up and spend some time with it before we call them."

"It?" she questioned, since last time when she had woken up, he had already named their baby and had been bonding with him for an hour, which had to be why Tuff was such a daddy's boy.

"I asked them not to tell me. We will find out together."

"Captain, did you really wait for me?"

"Of course, I did. You passing out last time had been a surprise, so this time, I was prepared. I love you, Dylan Marquez. Now push the call button, and let's meet our baby."

Moments later, a grinning Elissa came in, pushing the little bed that babies sleep in while at the hospital. Dylan knew she had been in the OR the entire time the baby had been born, even if she barely remembered it. Elissa picked up the baby and handed it to Dylan with a wink. "Another cute one, guys."

"You looked, didn't you?" Holden asked, pressing his lips into a thin line.

"Of course, I looked! I'm a professional." Then she turned and walked out of the room without telling them anything else.

In her arms, the baby looked exactly like Tim and Tuff. That was okay because they mostly looked like their dad. No matter how many times she looked at her own baby pictures, Dylan thought Tim and Tuff looked very little like her.

Unwrapping the blankets was enough to make the little thing's lip quiver. Beside her, Holden whispered, "Tucker."

"I don't see him as a Tucker. Brady."

"I think you said that one for Tuff, and I'm still not feeling it," he argued, touching the little hand that had started to flail.

"Well, we can't *not* name him," Dylan agued back. With the blanket gone, the baby's skinny legs stretched out, enjoying the room for the first time in its short life.

"Tom."

"Tim and Tom? That would just be fun for the rest of our lives." She gently slapped his arm at the suggestion. She was sure he wasn't even trying anymore.

"Tennyson."

"Ten?"

"Nope, just Tennyson, no nickname. Just Tennyson."

Dylan looked back at their baby. "I like it. Why didn't you say that one three months ago?"

Holden shrugged. "I just thought of it now. He looks like a Tennyson."

"He does." She picked up the baby carefully and looked into the eyes of Tennyson Marquez. It was perfect.

Together they looked over their perfect baby, with hair standing on end and arms and legs slowly stretching.

"Have you picked a name yet?" A nurse rushed in and checked on the monitors that were still attached to Dylan.

"Tennyson," Holden informed her with a smile.

"Tennyson is adorable for a girl. Elissa said you'd go with Talia."

"Girl?" Dylan looked at the nurse as if she was speaking a different language. They hadn't even looked, just assumed that it was another boy.

"Yup, a girl. Didn't you even look?" The nurse asked as she made notes in a notebook, not looking at them at all.

"We just assumed it was another boy! We have boys." Dylan looked at the baby again—their baby girl.

"Well, now you have a girl. Still going with Tennyson then?" She finally looked up from her paperwork and smiled at the little family.

Dylan looked at Holden and grinned. "Yes," they said together.

Their rough-and-tumble household was going to be different now. Their little girl looked at them both and gave them a crooked smile. It might have just been gas, but Dylan was sure Tennyson knew that everything was about to change around the Marquez house forever.

ABOUT ME, ALIE GARNETT

I love to read and prefer a little spice in those books. I am lucky enough to live on a small hobby farm in northern Minnesota with her husband and two kids. I enjoy spending time in the pasture with my two mini horses and one fainting goat (who doesn't actually faint). When I'm not writing, I'm busy trying to do all the things I didn't get to while writing. Or maybe I wouldn't have gotten to them anyway, because its laundry, dishes and fun things like that.

ALSO BY ALIE GARNETT

<u>Landstad, ND</u>

Invisible

Irresistible

Impulsive

Insuppressible

Intriguing

Imperfect

Irreplaceable

<u>The Great Lovely Falls</u>

Falling for the Single Mom

Falling for his Best Friends Sister

Falling for the Boss

Falling for his Step-Sister

Falling for his Fake Wife

Falling into a Second Chance

<u>Hart Series</u>

Seeing her Pain

Her Favor

Max Valentine is Looking at Me!

Keeping her Safe

<u>Stand Alone</u>

Romancing the Doctor

www.ingramcontent.com/pod-product-compliance
Lightning Source LLC
Chambersburg PA
CBHW070352200726
48294CB00003B/860